DIANE WILLIAMS GORDON

Ruby Hope Valley

Black Rose Writing | Texas

First printing

ISBN: 978-1-68433-163-5

PUBLISHED BY BLACK ROSE WRITING
www.blackrosewriting.com
Printed in the United States of America

Suggested Retail Price (SRP) $16.95

Ruby Hope Valley is printed in Palatino Linotype

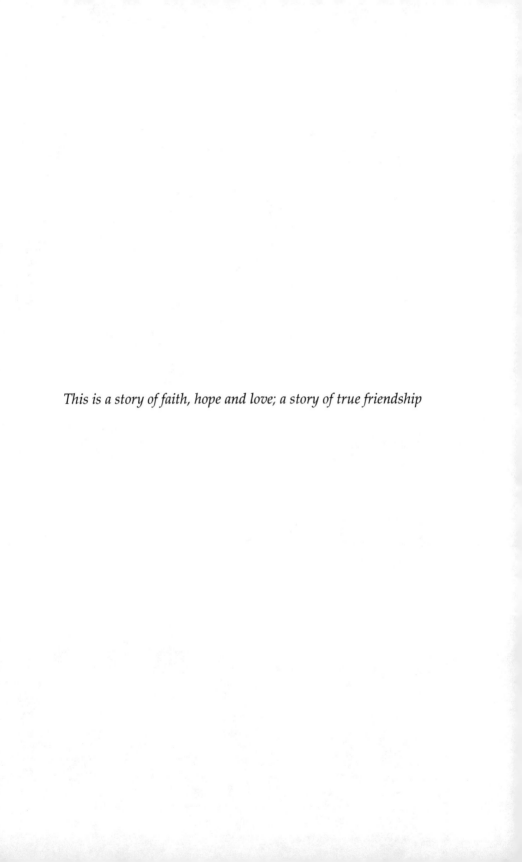

This is a story of faith, hope and love; a story of true friendship

Ruby Hope Valley

Prologue

It was a cold, windy day in November 1975, when a thoughtful, caring Christian woman,

Betty Anne Miller was invited to come and join the Amish women's Quilting group. She had often gone out to the community to care for the elderly and became a trusted friend.

She lives in the beautiful little town of Ruby Hope Valley. She carries a hurtful secret in her heart until she meets a young Amish girl named Sara Jane King. The two women share their love of family and lifelong friendship together.

"The secrets we keep in our hearts sometimes spill over into despair. We want to tell someone so badly but keep it hidden there."

Chapter One

Betty Anne Miller was a very lonely retired nurse in her late 50's who volunteered at the local hospital flower shop in Ruby Hope Valley. She had two children, twins, Danny and Sadie.

The twins longed for more out of life than the small town could give them. So, at the age of 18 they left for the city and never returned. She has struggled for many years trying to understand why they left. She longed to hear from them but feared they might never return. She kept it to herself and carried her secret around in heart. She loved living in Ruby Hope and wanted to spend the rest of her days there.

She enjoyed being around the Amish people who lived on the outskirts of town. They were plain and simple and always there for each other in times of need. They weren't greedy or selfish and worked hard every day. The Amish women invited her to join them in the quilting group; she was excited and couldn't wait to go. The ladies would meet at one of the women's homes and sit around the table and talk of ordinary things, such as canning, recipes, and baking. She had never quilted before but was anxious to learn how they pieced the fabrics together. There was a delicious aroma from the cookies and cakes they had been baking. And they always had fresh bread on the table.

In November 1975 when winter came to Ruby Hope everyone bundled up like Eskimos. Snow covered everything. The winds were so strong you could hardly see where you were going. She worried about her Amish friends and wanted to go out to the Community to check on them. The Amish men stock piled wood all year long and stored it next to the house. The warmth from the fireplace always kept their homes warm and cozy. You could see the smoke coming from their chimneys for miles. Whenever someone in the Community needed to build a barn or house they came together and supported each other. In that same spirit, Betty Anne wanted to be there for her new friends.

The storm had just about crippled the whole county, and the beautiful green fields were covered with snow. The barn roofs were so heavy people worried that they might cave in. The horses, cows, and chickens were all kept inside the barn during bad days. It was hard work keeping them all fed and warm during the cold days of winter, but the men would get up at 4 am every morning and trudge through the snow to get to the barn.

They had wood burning stoves in the barn that they lit as soon as they got inside; they worked all day taking care of the animals. It didn't matter how cold it was or how much snow was on the ground, these men worked hard. When it was time for lunch, the women of the house rang a bell, so the fathers and sons could hear it and come in for lunch. The Amish women also worked hard, cleaning, baking, and sewing.

December came, and it was Christmas time in Ruby Hope Valley. The cold weather didn't let up, but no one seemed to care. They still ran around trying to get their Christmas shopping done. Betty Anne missed going out to the Amish Community and wished it would stop snowing. Everywhere you looked, Christmas lights shone through the windows of the big old houses. The trees that lined the streets sparkled with colorful lights and glistened with snow. The store fronts had beautiful decorations in all their windows.

When the snow momentarily paused, she said, "Thank goodness the snow has stopped coming down. I should try to go Christmas shopping. I truly want to go to the tree lighting on Christmas Eve." She went into town to do her shopping but couldn't stop thinking about her Amish friends, so she decided to drive out to the town. The roads were covered with snow and ice, as she drove slowly to avoid an accident. She wondered if they celebrated Christmas. She decided to stop by the school house first. As she walked into the one room school house, the children were reading a story about Christmas. She stopped and smiled as she watched the excitement on their sweet little faces.

After she left the school, she drove down the dirt road that led to the Amish Community.

She didn't see any Christmas lights coming from their homes, but she did see large wreaths hanging on the front doors. As she drove home she couldn't stop thinking about how calm and peaceful the community was. She said to herself, "I know they have big families and will all be together on Christmas day; and I will be lonely."

Chapter Two

Christmas Eve arrived, and Betty Anne went into town to watch the tree lighting.

The big tree sat right in the middle of Ruby Hope's town square. No one seemed to care how cold it was or how much snow was on the ground. It was Christmas and the excitement in the air was overwhelming. She began to wonder where her children were and what they were doing on this Christmas Eve. She wished they were here in the Valley with her, as she said a silent prayer: "Please God bring my son and daughter home one day. I miss them so much and need them in my life."

After Christmas the Amish women began having their sewing groups again. They met at one of the women's homes at least once a week. Betty Anne could just imagine the women sitting around a quilting frame on just such a winters day. Enjoying their hot tea and friendships.

Catching up on all the Amish community news and chatting about recipes and the way they prepared certain dishes. It takes a lot of patience to be able to put the quilting pieces together, but these women were experts at quilting. She was a little uncertain about it, but she wanted to try and learn.

The weather remained very cold, and the ground was scattered with leaves and debris.

But inside Nellie Mae's house the wood stove created an inviting warmth. She had been baking apple pies and oatmeal cookies that morning, and the house was filled with a scent of cinnamon.

Her heart filled with love for these women; she felt so at home in their presence.

She became good at quilting; most of all she loved the interaction with the women. The colors they used seemed conservative in style; the solids of blue, brown, and black made them look a little dull to her. This was to be a wedding quilt for Sara Jane King, who was getting married in the spring. Nellie Mae said, "I suggest we use more piecing and add some additional colors to the quilt. We should add dark red and maybe olive green; this will make it more attractive." Betty Anne was amazed at the workmanship that went into the quilting. She said, "I know this quilt is going to be beautiful no matter what colors are used."

Sara Jane King was to marry a nice young Amish man named Levi Click. She was helping to work on her wedding quilt, and she said, "I have decided on the wedding ring quilt. I want lots of colors in it. Even if the colors are dark I just know the quilt will be lovely."

Betty Anne and Sara Jane became friends and always sat together at the quilting. Sara Jane explained a little to her about the quilting bees. She said, "Many women would work on their quilts in the winter months on one's own. Then they came up with the idea of getting together to quilt. This was much better for everyone. They would each contribute pieces of material and end up with a beautiful quilt. I heard the quilting bees are going to start getting together in the spring. It would be much better for everyone.

Betty Ann said, "You remind me a little of my own daughter, Sadie." She replied, "My mother passed away when I was just ten years old. I truly miss her." She felt a closeness to Betty Anne and began to think of her as a mother figure. She continued, "I have three brothers, Caleb, Matthew, and the youngest, John. They help my Dad on the farm. I'm responsible for all the cooking for the family. Caleb and Matthew are married, but my brother John still lives at home." "You're so lucky to have your brothers," She said. "I'm on my own in town, except for my friend and neighbor, Barbara Cummings. She comes over to make sure I'm ok from time to time. My two children, Danny and Sadie, left years ago, and I don't ever hear from them."

"I'm so sorry, Betty Anne. I hope we can always be friends. You're welcome to come to our home whenever you want to." Sara Jane continued to tell her about her family. "Dad and my brothers built on an addition to the main house for my grandparents, Ruth and Abram; which we call the Daudi Haus. It's an extension to our house." My grandparents are such a comfort to me, and I love the fact we live so close together. Grandmother Ruth is an expert when it comes to cooking food; she has raised four sons in her time, and she has had a lot of cooking experience. She is beginning to slow down, though, because she's getting up in age. "There's always cleaning, baking, and planting to do, so I am well prepared for marriage. I know when I get married I will have to take care of my husband and our new home in the same way. I'm already a good cook and always baking cakes and pies. When I leave home my older brother Caleb and his family will move into the big house and continue to take care of Dad and John."

Chapter Three

Up north of the community was a big covered flea market where a lot of the Amish people went on weekends to sell baked goods, quilts, and furniture they had made. Sara Jane decided she wanted to start selling her cakes at the market too. Her father (Mark) was not pleased about her going alone. She came up with the idea to ask Betty Anne if she would like to go. At the next quilting, she said, "Betty Anne, I have a great idea, and I hope you will agree with me. I want to sell my cakes at the big flea market. Dad says I should not go unaccompanied, and I thought you might like to go with me." She loved the idea. "It sounds like fun! I would love to go. I'll come over Saturday morning and help you get everything ready." Sara Jane baked several cakes. The aroma from the kitchen was enticing and lingered all day.

She kept baking as Betty Anne frosted the ones that had cooled. Sara Jane made a delicious frosting from some recipes she found that belonged to her mother. She said, "I found all kinds of recipes that belonged to my Mother in our old china cabinet. Every time I use one, I feel closer to her."

Betty Anne had arrived early, so she could assist Sara Jane in loading up the cakes. She knew the Amish didn't have cars, and Mark was against them. He said. "Sara Jane, you can drive the carriage today." "It would be easier to drive the car there, Mark," replied Betty Anne. He wasn't very pleased about the car, but he decided since she liked her so much he would allow it.

As Betty Anne drove up north of the county to market, she asked her if she knew where her son and daughter were. She was reluctant to talk about them. She had never spoken about them to anyone before, but since it was Sara Jane, she decided to tell her all about them.

She said, "My husband died many years ago in Vietnam, and I had to raise my son and daughter by myself. They resented me when they were growing up because they wanted things that I couldn't give them; they left Ruby Hope when they turned eighteen." She had tears in her eyes after hearing the story. "I just can't understand how they could treat you that way. I have longed my whole life to have a mother, and your two kids just left you without a word?" Both women had tears in their eyes but tried to hide them from each other.

They pulled up in front of the big market and were surprised to see so many people there.

She said, "Sara Jane, you won't have any problems selling those cakes of yours! Just look how many people are here today." They walked all around the flea market and admired the furniture and quilts on display. Sara Jane said. "I just had a flashback of when I was eight or nine years old. Mother brought me here once or twice before she died of cancer. I was too young to understand how sick she was, but I remember how we walked all over the flea market and saw people she knew. She would stop and talk to them, it seemed for a very long time. I wish those days were here again, and I could be with her." A tear trickled down her cheek. She brushed it away quick.

The Amish men and women had made all sorts of furniture: beautiful tables and chairs, bed frames, and picture frames. Some of the younger Amish girls brought candies such as fudge to sell. Betty Anne and Sara Jane got their booth set up. They put the cakes on the counter and hoped people would stop by and buy them. Before they knew it, all the cakes were sold. Sara

Jane said happily, "I can hardly believe all the cakes are gone. I'm going to save my money and use it for my wedding. There are so many things I need for our new home." Betty Anne smiled.

"That is a wonderful idea, Sara Jane."

Sara Jane said. "Our people live very simply and do not furnish their homes very much, but there are a few things I could use. I have a hope chest in my bedroom full of quilts, bed linens, dollies, and some pots and pans. Our neighbors from all over the Amish community have been giving me things for the past few months, ever since they found out I was getting married in the spring. You see, I'm older than most Amish girls when they marry, and I really thought I would never find someone I cared about. Then I met Levi

Click. He is a wonderful man. Levi says he's ready to settle down and start a family."

Chapter Four

Early one morning as Sara Jane was looking out the kitchen window she saw her

Dad walking across the lawn; his head was down. She had a horrible feeling in the pit of her stomach that something was wrong. She met him at the back door as he took off his boots and hung his hat. She said, "What's wrong? "One of the horses has died, daughter, and I'm not sure what has caused it; but it was the main horse Susie, we used to pull our buggy." She couldn't believe it. "Oh, Dad what do you think caused it?" He shook his head. "I'm going to call in a vet to examine the horse. I want to know why it died."

The Amish community's veterinarian Jim Peterson lived close by and would come out and check on the animals. Later that day they got news that one of the farms down the road lost some of their chickens. This alarmed Sara Jane's father when he heard the news. Mark said, "I'm afraid that a disease may be going around; there was no reason for our horse to die. The horse has always been in good health." The veterinarian came the following day to check on the horse. In the meantime, Dad covered the horse in a tarp.

The vet had bad news for Mark and nothing was the same after that. The Veterinarian said. "There is a disease going around, and it may affect all the animals in the barn. I will give you some liquid medicine to use in the other animals' food supply. I think it has something to do with the wheat the horses are eating. You should throw all of it out right away." Mark was upset and didn't know what to do. The vet pressed him: "You need to get together with the other farmers in the community and have the wheat tested." Mark knew he had to feed the other horses, but wasn't sure where he should go buy the wheat. And if the wheat was bad, other horses would die on other farms; he had to get the word out.

In the future, where was he going to go to buy more wheat for his horses? Mark called an emergency meeting of all the farmers. He told them, "We should throw out all the wheat we have. So far, no other horses have gotten sick; but we need to brace for the worst. It's just a matter of time before the other animals will become ill or die. We should all go to Ruby Hope and confront the store where we bought the wheat."

The men hitched up their horses to their buggies and headed to town, forming a convoy.

It was a sight when all the Amish buggies came into town. One after another they came. When they approached the store owners, they were surprised to find out that they already knew about the wheat and they were trying to get more wheat for the farmers. Everybody's tempers were in high gear that day, and the store owners were trying to explain to them what they were going to do about it. Everyone including the Amish men was yelling and talking at the same time. Once again, the people of Ruby Hope came together. The store manager said, "We have contacted the distributors of the wheat union, and we're waiting for them to arrive. Some of the other farmers around Ruby Hope have had some of their animals get sick from the same wheat."

Ultimately, several trucks drove into town loaded down with fresh wheat. Their drivers began giving out wheat bales to all the farmers, assuring them that the wheat was good.

Sara Jane's father could simply take the men's word for it. He knew he had to feed his other horses, and he didn't have any other choice. That night at dinner a special prayer went up for all the farmers and their animals. Mark prayed. "I pray that the new wheat will prove good, and no more animals will die."

The following day all his animals seemed to be ok, but during the night another horse died. Mark said, "Maybe the horse was already sick, or the new wheat was bad too. In any case,

I hope and pray that all the other animals will be ok." In the days and weeks to follow, the animals seemed to survive that horrible ordeal. The store manager told him the farm that supplied the tainted wheat was being sued. He vowed, "From now on the wheat will be examined before it's sold in the store." Sara Jane said, "That's the way it is in Ruby Hope. We stand together in times of crisis."

Note: Oak and the issues of cross contamination with wheat.

A post by Steve Martin who has a B.S. in Milling Science.

The grain storage/transporting infrastructure in the US virtually promises cross contamination of grains. Cleaning processes can separate grains with large size and shape differences at the

Flourmill. The wheat comes in about 0.5 corn and soybeans mixed in, but because of the size difference, they are easy to remove. Oats and wheat, on the other hand, are close to the same size and much difficult to remove.

Chapter Five

The cold weather didn't seem to be letting up. The frost on the window panes showed signs of a long cold winter. She just knew spring was right around the corner. She couldn't wait to start final preparations for her wedding. She only saw Levi once a week; he worked on a farm that was located fifty miles away from the Community. He came home on the weekends. During this time Levi started thinking about his job. He said to himself, "I don't mind the drive so much now. But after we get married, Sara Jane wouldn't want me to be gone all the time. Besides she would want to stay close to her family. I'm a black smith; I shouldn't have a hard time getting a job. Maybe my boss would give me a recommendation." Levi didn't sleep much that night. He tossed and turned all night thinking about what he was going to do.

On Sunday, Sara Jane got up early, washed and dressed herself, and ran downstairs. She knew she had to get breakfast going. She lit the wood stove as she always did. Grandmother and grandpa came over and poured the milk for everyone. Her brothers, Caleb and Mathew, would be going to church with their families today, so they wouldn't be here for breakfast. John wasn't married yet so there would be Dad, John, Grandmother, Grandpa, and Sara Jane.

She set the table for five people and finished cooking the pancakes. Dad and John had gotten up hours ago and were in the barn feeding the animals. They came inside through the back porch took their boots off and hung their coats and hats up. They sat down at the table and lowered their heads in silent prayer. The January winds whipped and sang around the windows as they began to eat. She had built a big fire in the fireplace earlier, and it was roaring. She began thinking to herself: "This fireplace was built out of the stones the Amish men in the community dug out of the ground when they were building the house;

it covers one whole side of the sitting room. It's so big and keeps this old house cozy and warm."

After breakfast, the family was ready to go to church. Mark and John had already hitched the horses. They would drive the enclosed buggy today; it was way too cold to ride in an open one. The ground was hard with snow and ice and made it hard for the horses to trot on. Dad said, "Be sure to wrap yourselves up with those blankets in the buggy; it's colder than it has been." The clip clop of the horses' feet and the buggy wheels on the snow and ice was all they could hear. When they arrived at the church, she saw Levi and waved to him. The men sat on one side of the room and the women sat on the other side.

After preaching the women folk set up the food on a long table. They put out potato salad, fried chicken, several casseroles, breads, and rolls. The women and children went first to make their plates; then the men came in. She went into the church and found a bench to sit on. Levi came over and sat next to her. They talked of ordinary things. Sara Jane said. "Levi, could you come over for supper this evening? I know you will be leaving early tomorrow, and we won't see each other till next weekend." "Yes, I would love to, Sara Jane," he replied.

After church the family rode home with Dad at the reins again. Arriving home, he and John unhitched the horses and led them to the barn. Sara Jane took a roast out of the icebox and got it prepared to cook. She wanted to have a very special dinner that evening for Levi. She would boil potatoes, have corn on the cob and string beans. She said, "Dad may I use the best dishes for dinner tonight? Levi is coming over, and I want the table to look its best." He nodded. "Yes daughter, whatever you want to do."

Levi showed up at 7 p.m. dressed in his best suit and holding a bunch of beautiful flowers. She was so proud of the way he looked and happy to see him. They all had dinner and then went into the sitting room to talk. Dad lit his pipe and relaxed in his favorite chair.

Levi and Sara Jane sat on the sofa together. The warmth from the fireplace was so inviting.

Her grandparents excused themselves and went to their part of the house; they were tired and ready for bed. John went up to his room to read his Bible before going to sleep.

Levi said, "Sara Jane, we need to find time to look for a small house. With me working out of town it's difficult for me to give much time to this search. Maybe you could look around and see if you can find us a house. We need a place with a little land and a barn." She nodded. "I want a big front porch and a small place to plant some flowers too."

Chapter Six

The days that followed made it very difficult to get outside. A winter storm had hit the town. Freezing rain was falling, and the roads were scattered with debris. Sara Jane liked to read, so sometimes she would curl up on her bed and read a book. The house was a little cold, but she kept as much wood burning as she could. John had stacked the firewood on the front porch so, she wouldn't have to go so far to get it.

The fields were snowy white, and everything looked serene and quiet outside. Sara Jane looked out her bedroom window and wished for spring to hurry and get there. She wanted to go outside and plant flowers and run through the soft green grass in her bare feet. She said, "Oh, how I long to smell the fresh air of spring coming in through the windows."

She suddenly thought of Grandmother Ruth and Grandpa Abram. "I wonder if they are warm enough?" She decided to go check on them. She tapped on their door and got no answer at first, so she tapped again. Grandpa opened the door with a sad look on his face.

"Grandpa, what's wrong?" "Grandmother isn't feeling very well." She promptly went to see about her. "How do you feel today, Grandmother?" Sara Jane touched the older woman's cheek, checking her head for fever. "Grandpa, she needs a doctor. It's so cold outside I don't know if anyone can get the doctor here in this weather." She placed a cold washcloth on her forehead. "Grandmother, you need to drink some water. I'm afraid you might get dehydrated if you don't drink fluids."

After she did what she could for her, she ran over to her side of the house and got her boots and coat on. She crossed the yard and walked to the barn where she found Mark. She said.

"Dad, Grandmother is running a high fever. We need doctor

Graber. Could you go and get him?"

"Don't worry, daughter, we will get the doctor and bring him back." Mark and John got the horse out of the barn and hitched him up to the carriage. The temperature was still very low, but the freezing rain and snow had stopped. They put a quilt over the horse to keep her warm.

They traveled as fast as they could, but the road was treacherous. The ground was muddy and slippery, which made it difficult for the horse to pull the buggy. At last they arrived at doctor Graber's home office. Mark said, "Doctor Graber--- could you go back with us to check on my mother. She's very sick." The doctor retrieved his bag, coat, and boots. Mark worried about Ruth. She had always been a strong healthy woman, but recently. at the age of seventy-eight, he had noticed she was slowing down some.

When they returned, doctor Graber got out of the buggy and ran around to the back porch. He removed his boots and coat and found Sara Jane in the kitchen waiting for him.

She offered him a hot cup of tea. He drank a little of the tea and thanked her, then went straight to see Ruth. When he came out of her room, he said, "She is burning up with a temperature and her blood pressure is elevated. I believe she has pneumonia and needs to go to the hospital."

Mark was reluctant. He said, "I don't want her out in this weather. We will do everything for her here at home; I don't think she should be moved." The doctor was used to this attitude. He nodded. "I will come around each day and check on Ruth; if she gets any worse, though, please send someone to get me right away." He gave them some liquid medication to give her every two hours until the fever went away, instructing them, "Keep her as warm as you can and give her plenty of liquids." Sara Jane was very worried and decided she would stay as close as she could to her. She also had a thought: "maybe Betty Anne could come and stay with her?" But then she considered the weather and the roads might prevent her friend from getting there.

She put on her boots and coat and ran down to the barn to talk to her father about Betty Anne. Mark said. "I'm not happy about that idea.

We can handle it on our own." She pleaded, "But Dad, I do all the cooking and baking, and I don't have time to sit with her. It would be a big relief if she could come out." "Alright, daughter, you can have your friend come stay with Grandmother Ruth. She may have a hard time getting here, though."

She added her headscarf, wrapping it partly around her face for protection against the cold and ran down the road as fast as she could. The telephone booth was in a field near the farm. The phone booth had been installed there for the Amish Community emergencies. She called Betty Anne's home phone and told her about Ruth. She asked, "Betty Anne, could you come out to the farm and watch over Grandmother Ruth? She is sick, and we need your support." "I'm more than happy to help," She assured her, "but I'm worried about ice on the road." *She thought to herself, "What if my car won't make it?"*

Chapter Seven

The next morning the weather began to improve, and Sara Jane was relieved.

Betty Anne was going to be able to make it after all. Her little grandmother was still gravely ill, but she knew that she would be able to give her assistance. She had taken care of many of the elderly people in their community; she had a lot of faith in her. She had many aunts who could come over and stay with her, but her first thought was Betty

Anne. She thought the world of her and trusted her to do the right thing for her grandmother.

Mark was still a little leery of all this, but he knew Sara Jane had Ruth's health at heart.

He trusted his daughter's judgment. To others he seemed stern, but in his heart, he was as any child worried about his parents. Mark prayed. "Please let my mother get well, Lord."

Shortly after noon Betty Anne left for Sara Jane's house. The roads had melting ice and snow on them but were passable. She just took her time driving and tried to be as careful as she could. The daylight lasted longer than it had lately, and the freezing rain had stopped. When she finally arrived, Mark met her in the driveway of their house. He helped her out of the car, and said, "Thank you for assisting us." "Oh, I am happy to do what I can for grandmother Ruth.

I'm sure she will be fine, so don't you worry about her. I will take good care of her." Mark said, "The ground is wet and muddy, so let me escort you to the back door of our enclosed porch. You can hang your coat there and take off your boots."

Sara Jane was in the kitchen preparing lunch for the family when she came in the back door. She offered her a cup of hot tea and a slice of apple pie. She sat down for a spell and said. "How is your

Grandmother doing? What has been done for her?" Sara Jane said, "We want her to be well. Grandpa Abram is a nervous wreck, and you must overlook his hovering. It is because he is so worried. The doctor said she has pneumonia and should be in the hospital, but Dad doesn't want to move her in this weather. Dr. Graber left some medicine for her." She understood and said. "Don't worry; I will take good care of Grandmother and Grandpa."

She enjoyed the tea and pie, then said, "I'm ready to see Ruth." Sara Jane took her over and introduced her to Grandpa Abram. He seemed delighted to meet her and sat down in a chair in the corner of the room. She felt Ruth's forehead to see if her fever had gone away yet. She seemed to be cool. "Are you able to eat a little soup for me? Ruth said, "I'm not very hungry, but I will try to eat a little." After the soup, she washed the sick woman's face and arms and put a clean gown on her. She fluffed her pillows and set her up a little in bed. Ruth said, "I feel much better. I appreciate you coming out to take care of me. I have heard about you through some of the other Amish women; everything I heard was nice." She thanked her and smiled to herself.

After Ruth had sat up in bed for a period, she said, "Ruth, you should lie down and take a little nap." She continued to keep watch over her for several days. Ruth was getting stronger and felt so much better. Mark came over to see her, and she was very happy to see him. Betty Anne told him, "She's getting stronger, and I believe she is going to come through this. I've always heard Amish women were survivors and hardworking.

I know she has worked hard her whole life, and she has a strong will to live. I believe she is going to be ok."

Betty Anne stayed for almost a week, then decided it was time to go home. Sara Jane truly hated to see her leave and invited her to come out to visit them whenever she wanted.

Mark shook her hand and thanked her again for taking care of his mother. As she drove back to Ruby Hope, she pondered the last week of her life. She thought, "Sara Jane's family are very nice people; I truly enjoyed being around them. They live simply, and everything they have means so much to them." She reflected that their family, land, animals, and crops were all they cared about. They didn't need fancy clothes; they were happy with plain and simple.

That night, Sara Jane decided she would make a special dinner for her Grandparents.

She fried chicken, made gravy and biscuits, corn on the cob, and string beans. After everything was prepared, Ruth and Abram came over from their place. Grandmother said, "I feel so good I think I could eat a whole cow." They all laughed at her, and Dad said, "Well, Grandmother

Ruth is her old self again." The family was beginning to heal.

Chapter Eight

The winter months began to fade away, and the sunshine began to last longer. The days were growing longer, and the beginning of flowers emerged from the ground. Spring was in the air. Sara Jane and Levi were looking ahead to their wedding. She had searched for a little house and thought she found the perfect one; Levi still had to look at it. She told her father, "It has two bedrooms a family room and kitchen, Dad." It also has a small barn out back which Levi can build onto if he wants to make it bigger; and a lovely yard. I can make a flower garden and grow some blueberries. I can hardly wait for Levi to see it." Mark was excited for her and thought the house sounded wonderful.

They planned to have the wedding at Sara Jane's house in April of 1976. Normally Amish have their weddings at another relative's home, but she wanted to have it at her own home instead. She wanted to invite Betty Anne to her wedding but needed to speak with the Bishop first.

Bishop Isaac was a kind and understanding man. He knew of Betty Anne's reputation and how she had made Grandmother Ruth well again. Sara Jane said. "I think the world of her, and I truly would love for her to come to my wedding." Bishop Isaac was hesitant in his remarks and said. "It isn't our custom to have people from the outside come to our weddings; but outsiders are welcome to attend the lunch after the wedding. I will call a meeting of the elders and see what their thoughts are. I will let you know their decision as soon as I can." She wanted to contact her and invite her to the wedding as soon as she could. She had to be content with his answer for the time being.

In the meantime, she focused her attention on getting the house ready for the wedding.

She wrote down all the things that she needed to do. The following morning, she strolled down the road to the phone booth and called her two cousins, Susan and Mary. The girls were Mennonite and had gone to more modern things such as a phone in their home. She knew they would come out to the house and assist her with the cleaning. Unexpectedly after all the waiting, her wedding day was coming up, the Sunday after next.

Susan and Mary arrived on Tuesday and began scrubbing the walls and floors. They removed the everyday furniture from the sitting room and brought in benches for people to sit on. They put them up against the walls until time to put them in place. In the middle of the room they placed a smaller bench that would hold a floral arrangement with a candle on each side. They went ahead and placed the candles on the bench.

She remembered she needed to tell all the bridesmaids what the colors were going to be so they would be able to get their dresses ready in time. The bridesmaids in the wedding party were to wear purple dresses, and the groomsmen would have on purple shirts under their black suits. It was their custom for everyone who participated in the wedding to wear the same colors. She decided to ask the relatives who were serving the lunch to wear lavender. This way they would blend in with the wedding party. It was all so exciting she could hardly sleep at night just thinking about it. Her new purple dress with its white starched apron and white kappa would be so lovely along with all the others.

When Levi came home on Friday evening, he stopped at Sara Jane's house, and she told him excitedly, "Levi, I found a farm house that I want you to see Saturday." So, the next morning Levi came with his horse and buggy and picked her up. They spoke of the wedding and the little house. As they pulled up into the driveway, she said, "I hope you will like the house."

Levi spotted the small barn out back, and said, "The barn is awfully small, but I can build onto it one day. I am surprised at how small the house is, but I think it will be perfect for us. At least until I can build a larger one."

Normally, in the Amish community, the bride and groom live with the parents of the bride, but Sara Jane and Levi wanted to start their new lives on their own. Levi said, "I like the place. I'll get the information about the house and see if we can purchase it."

Chapter Nine

As they backed the horse and buggy out of the drive way, they saw a car coming their way. The man driving the car was going way too fast, and their horse began to buck and kick, making the buggy swerve and turn over. Sara Jane was thrown out of the buggy and into a ditch face down. Levi hit his head on the front of the buggy and was dizzy and confused. He looked around and screamed for her. Then he crawled out of the buggy and landed on the ground. He was half conscious as he crawled, trying to find her.

He momentarily saw her and made his way over to where she was lying. He tried to pick her up, but she was dead weight. Two neighbor men rode by and saw the accident. They jumped down from their buggy and ran over to Levi and Sara Jane. She was unconscious and bleeding from her head. They lifted her and put her in the buggy. The man said. "Do you want us to take her to the hospital?" "Yes, thank you," he said. "I will go with you."

They situated the couple's horse and buggy against the fence, and then took them to the hospital in their buggy. They pulled their horse and buggy up to the emergency entrance. Levi yelled, "Please help us. A car hit our buggy, and my friend is hurt really bad." EMTs ran out with a stretcher and placed her on it, then rushed her into the building. Levi said, "Thank you both for your assistance; you'll have been so kind." One of the men said, "We'll let Mark know what happened and return your buggy to the farm."

One of the Amish gentlemen said, "there have been too many of these accidents with us.

People drive way too fast and there should be something we can do about it. We have stop lights on the back of the buggies, but most people don't pay attention to that. We are so sorry Levi that this happened to you and your friend. We will be praying for both of you.

Levi was so grateful to the two men. He walked into the hospital and spoke with the doctor who was treating her. The doctor said, "The young lady has a fracture on her head and is unconscious. She could be like this for several days. You should just take a seat in the waiting room and someone will come and get you if there is any change." Levi found a seat in the waiting room. He sat down and began to pray: "God, please help Sara Jane recover from this terrible accident. I feel so lonesome right now and need someone to come and comfort me."

Before long Mark and John came through the emergency room doors. Mark had a very worried look on his face. John whispered to Levi. "Levi, please tell us, is Sara Jane going to be ok? He just looked at John and said, "You'll need to pray hard for her John, she's not doing so well. A car ran us off the road, and she was thrown out of the buggy and landed in a ditch. The doctor said she has a fracture on her head. She could be unconscious for several days. He said all we can do is wait." They sat silently as if they were praying.

They stayed all night in the emergency room, sitting or pacing the floors. The next morning they heard a voice call out to Mark, it was Betty Anne. She was on her way to work in the flower shop when she saw them; she stopped and asked what had happened. They explained about Sara Jane, and she was in shock. Tears were running down her face, and she began shaking. They asked her to sit down and calm herself for a bit. She just couldn't believe what happened and was worried to about her. She told them that she needed to let the other lady in the flower shop know she wasn't working that day, and she would be right back.

She came back just a few minutes later and stayed with them. Around 4:00 in the afternoon, the doctor came out to give them some news. He told them that she had not woke up and that they should go home and try to get some rest. He said that it might take several days before she regained consciousness. None of the men wanted to leave, but John and

Mark knew they needed to go home and check on the animals and let Grandmother Ruth and

Grandpa Abram know what had happened. Levi didn't want to leave, but Betty Anne assured him that she would stay there until he came back. All three men got into Mark's buggy and went home.

Chapter Ten

When they arrived back at the farm, John took the horse and buggy to the barn and told his Dad and Levi to go ahead and go inside the house. With heavy hearts, the men walked across the front lawn and around the house to the back door. They came through the back porch and hung their hats on the rack. As they came into the kitchen, Grandmother Ruth had supper warming on the stove for them. She knew something was wrong from the looks on their faces. Mark looked up at her and told them what happened and about Sara Jane. Grandpa Abram was sitting at the table as Grandmother Ruth begin shaking. You could see tears in their eyes, as she sat down at the table. She felt like her legs were going out from under her. John came in the back door and hung his hat up, and they sat down at the kitchen table.

She got up and put the food on the table and told them they needed to try and eat something to keep their strength up. She poured them a glass of water and sat down at the table with them. The men just sat there for a time as if they couldn't move; they were so worried about her. They soon ate a little and then decided to get a few hours of sleep and head back to the hospital very early in the morning.

Mark, John, and Levi returned to the hospital early the next morning. There was no change in Sara Jane, so all they could do was wait and pray. Barbara, Betty Anne's neighbor and friend, called her on the lobby phone and told her about the donations she received from the people in town. "Betty Anne, you were right about the people in this town. They have been calling all morning wanting to know how she is and donating money for her hospital expenses.

The mayor decided to have a prayer vigil for her too. Everyone held candles and prayed. It was very nice; I wish you could have been here."

The Amish community was meeting at the church, having their own prayer service for her. They had come together and cooked food for the family. Some of them came to the hospital to support them. There were so many horses and buggies parked in front of the hospital that the staff had to call a policeman to direct traffic. Barbara called Betty Anne again.

"We have raised five thousand dollars for Sara Jane's hospital bill, and the money is still coming in. I can't believe the generosity the town folks have shown toward this Amish girl." The situation was a little delicate. Mark wasn't the kind of man who took handouts. Betty Anne decided not to tell Mark about the donations. She would pay the hospital bill and not let him know anything about it; it would be an anonymous gift.

On the third day, she began to wake up. Doctor Cane couldn't believe all the Amish people in the waiting room. He said to Mark. "She has awakened, but she's not out of the woods just yet. She still needs to stay in the hospital for a few more days. She had a bad bump on her head, and we want to make sure there is no lasting damage to her brain; you and Levi can come in to see her for a few minutes."

Everyone was so excited to hear she had awakened and seemed to be doing ok.

Mark and Levi went in to see her. They were taken aback that she had a bandage on her head. A tear rolled down Mark's face as he walked up to the bed. She took his hand and said, "Am I going to be ok, Dad? Levi was standing on the other side of the bed and took her other hand in his. She squeezed his hand and held on to it. Mark looked at her and said. "Daughter, you are in God's hand now, and you are going to be just fine." She gave a half smile and closed her eyes, all the while holding on to Levi. He knew she would not be recovered enough in a week so they would have to change the date for the wedding.

Everyone in the waiting room was so relieved to know she had come out of the coma and decided to go home. The horses and buggies leaving the hospital were a sight to see. The buggies looked like a convoy going down the road. The policeman tried to direct traffic, so they could all go together. He held back the cars and trucks and let the horse-drawn vehicles go through the intersection and head out of town.

Betty Anne knew she needed to leave for a time too, so she said her goodbyes and prepared to go home. She wanted to talk to Barbara about the donations. She said, "Mark I will be back in the morning. If you need me here is my number." Mark and John knew that they needed to go and see about the animals, so they also returned home. Levi decided to stay a bit longer just in case she needed him. He stayed in her hospital room and sat silent as she slept.

Chapter Eleven

The following day Sara Jane was sitting up in the hospital bed. She looked like she felt better, so Levi decided to leave for a period. He thought about the little white house.

He would go talk to the owner about purchasing it. If they could make a deal, the house would be theirs. Thus resolved, he went to the man and made his offer. Levi and the owner agreed on a price. It all happened so fast, he could hardly wait to tell her.

When the Amish women heard about the house he had bought, they decided to get it ready for them. They scrubbed the floors and walls, swept the kitchen and front porch.

They even cleaned up the yard around the house. Levi thanked them profusely: "I can't believe what you ladies have done for us. I am so grateful, and I know she will be too. Thank you for your assistance. I think I will go buy some furniture for the house. We need a table, chairs, a bed, and a dresser." The women thought that was a good idea, and they asked Levi if there was anything else they could do for them. "You'll have done enough already; thank you again."

On the way toward town, he decided he would buy a bookcase for all her books. He thought an antique store would be the place to go. She would also want a china cabinet for the china her Mother had left her. It had never been used and was kept in the big china cabinet they had at home. Mark told her the china would be hers when she got married. He wanted to have the house all ready for her when she came home from the hospital. It would be a nice surprise for her when she was able to go see the house.

She subsequently came home after being kept under observation for several days in the hospital; her brain scan was normal. She was still supposed to rest for a few days. Levi had gone back to work, so she lay around the house for a few days then got up and begin cooking. Mark said, "Sara Jane, you need to rest longer." She gestured reassuringly, and said,

"Dad, I feel fine now, stop worrying about me."

More than ever now, Levi was thinking about trying to get a blacksmith job closer to home. He decided to go speak with his boss and see if he would give him a recommendation.

After what happened to Sara Jane, he didn't want to be so far away from her; particularly if something should happen again. His boss was very understanding and said, "Levi I will give you a great recommendation, but I really hate to lose you." Levi felt better about it now and thought he would put the word out around the Valley that he was pursuing a job as a metalworker.

It didn't take long for Levi to get some answers about a job. There were several big horse ranches around the town, and one was looking for a good blacksmith. Levi couldn't wait to tell Sara Jane that he had a prospect of a job close to home. Friday after Sara Jane had come home from the hospital, Levi came home from the ranch. He stopped to see her, and said "Sara Jane, I would like for you to take a ride with me; I want to show you something." She felt a little hesitant to ride in the buggy again because of the accident. He said, "Don't worry, I assure you I will be extra careful and take my time. I have a special surprise for you." She decided to go after all.

Levi helped her get into the buggy and told her they would be there in just a few minutes.

They were silent for a spell; all they could hear were the horse's hooves clip clopping on the dirt road. He told her, "I'm thinking about getting a job close to home. My boss has given me a good recommendation and I'm sure I will be able to get a job." "Oh, Levi it would nice to have you home instead of gone all the time."

They arrived at the white house again. Sara Jane was a bit nervous because the accident had happened right in front of the house. He gave her his hand, so she could step down from the buggy and opened the front door, to her surprise. "Go ahead and go inside Sara Jane, this is our new home." She felt a tear run down her face as she stepped inside the house. "When you were in the hospital, I went ahead and bought the house for us; I hope you will be happy here. A few of the neighborhood ladies came while you were in the hospital and cleaned the house for us."

Once Inside, she noticed the kitchen table and chairs. On the counter was a big bowl of fruit. She said, "It's so clean, and I love the furniture! Levi, did you pick it out?" He hesitated for a moment and said, "I did, I was hoping you would ask me that question."

As they walked through the house, she came to the bedroom and was surprised to see the bedroom furniture. "My wedding quilt will look beautiful on the bed!" she exclaimed. He took her hand and said. "I was so worried about you, Sara Jane." "I love the house and everything you've done. I can't wait for us to get married," She replied. He took her in his arms and told her how much he loved her. "I love you too, Levi, and I just know we will be happy here in our little home." They hugged each other and then continued to look around. They went outside and walked over to the barn. Levi thought maybe someday he would open his own blacksmith shop.

Chapter Twelve

As they got closer to the barn, it turned out to be bigger than they thought. There were some cracks in the walls, but those could be repaired. Levi said, "It will take a little work, but I think I can make a nice shop out of it." They felt very happy and just wanted to linger as long as they could. They walked around the house and sat on the porch steps for a spell, just day dreaming about what they could do with the place. She said, "It's getting late, Levi; I think we should start home." She thought to herself, *this has been a wonderful day.*

The following day, she wanted to call Betty Anne and thank her for staying at the hospital with her and tell her about their new house. She was so excited about everything.

She walked down the road to the outdoor phone booth and gave her a call. Betty Anne said, "I am so happy to hear from you, and I am happy for you and Levi. The house sounds beautiful, and I can't wait to see it, Sara Jane." She wanted to invite her to her wedding but she had not heard back from Bishop Isaac yet; so, she didn't mention it to her. She figured she would call again when she got the answer; that is, if the answer was yes. Her heart was aching to ask her friend, but she knew it might be impossible.

Around a week later they set another wedding day and time. Levi had already gotten a job on a horse ranch near Ruby Hope Valley. It was close enough so he would be home every night. "I am so happy about your new job, Levi. Could you come over and have supper with us?" "Yes, I would love to," he replied. After supper, they sat on the front porch and discussed their wedding plans. They decided on the first Saturday in May.

Sara Jane said. "The first Saturday in May is a beautiful time for a wedding. Let's go tell Dad."

Mark said. "I am delighted, and I guess you better get busy on the wedding plans, daughter."

The sitting room had already been cleaned and the benches brought in, so she simply had to tell everyone when the wedding would take place. She looked ahead to wearing her new purple dress with the starch white apron and her white kappa, and mused to herself, "Purple is my favorite color, and I just know it will be perfect for this time of the year." She opened her hope chest and took out some of her lace dollies and looked at them. She could almost imagine them in her new house and how pretty they were going to be. The wedding quilt was lying there, so lovely, and she could hardly wait to put it on their bed. She hugged it to her chest and closed her eyes while smiling to herself. She was thinking about Levi and what their life was going to be like together and how happy she was.

The next morning while cooking breakfast for the family, she heard a knock at the door. It was the Bishop; he had come to see her and give her his answer regarding Betty Anne.

She said, "Come in, Bishop Isaac, and have a cup of tea with us." He responded with a smile, "I would love some tea, Sara Jane." Grandmother Ruth and Granddaddy Abram came over from their place to give her a hand with breakfast, and Ruth said, "We are so delighted to see 'you, Bishop." They sat down at the table and shared tea with him. Grandmother Ruth said.

"Bishop Isaac, would you like to stay and have breakfast with us? You are more than welcome."

"No, thank you, I actually need to get on my way." He asked Sara Jane if she would see him to the front door. She was nervous, but she knew whatever the answer was, she would obey the rules.

Bishop Isaac said, "I had a meeting with the clergymen, and they all decided that because of all the good Betty Anne has done for the people in our community, they would bend the rules a little and let her attend the wedding." She was so excited that she gave the Bishop a big hug; he was taken aback but was happy for her too.

After breakfast and the dishes had all been washed and dried, she couldn't wait to call Betty Anne. She ran down the road to the outdoor phone booth and called her.

"Hi, Betty Anne, I am calling to invite you to my wedding. It's the first Saturday in May."

"I am so happy to be invited, Sara Jane. Thank you for asking me." She felt that everything was falling into place now, and she had never been happier than she was at that moment.

Chapter Thirteen

The wedding day ultimately came, and everyone in the house was rushing around trying to do last minute things. Grandmother Ruth said," I want to make sure we have plenty of cakes and cookies, and everything is laid out on the long table. The women are bringing several casseroles. Surely, we will have enough food for everyone to enjoy on this day." Sara Jane nodded. She was determined nothing was going to go wrong.

The day was bright and sunny, and all the flowers in the yard were blooming. She took note of this and said, "The Lord has made a beautiful day for our wedding; I am so grateful to him". She stopped in her tracks and said a silent prayer giving thanks for everything God had done for them. She looked so pretty in her purple Amish dress with the white starched apron.

Sara Jane said, "Dad, you look handsome in your Sunday suit and black straw hat; and you even shined your shoes. I am proud of you." He was a tall quiet man who loved his daughter and wanted the best for her. He liked Levi and thought he was a proper husband for his daughter. She continued approvingly, turning her attention to her brother. "John, you look nice in your black suit and purple shirt, too."

Her other two brothers and their families arrived early. Caleb and Matthew looked handsome in their black suits and purple shirts. She was so proud to have them in her ceremony as well as her sisters-in-law. Her wedding party included her three brothers and Levi's brother, Samuel, as well as her sisters-in-law, Maggie and Katherine. Her two cousins, Susan and Mary, were also her bridesmaids. Everyone looked lovely in their purple dresses. She wished she could preserve the sight of them with a picture, but they were not allowed to have cameras. Sara Jane thought, "It doesn't matter; the memory of the day will be in my heart for a long time."

Sara Jane and Levi had been married two years when she announced that they was going to have a baby. Mark was delighted and hugged his daughter with tears in his eyes.

He had six grandchildren already, but his single daughter was so special to him, and this was wonderful news. Over the past two years, Sara Jane and Betty Anne had become even closer.

Betty Anne came over to see the young couple quite often. When she learned that she was going to have a baby, she was very excited and happy for her. Betty Anne said. "Levi, I plan to buy a beautiful baby bed, but I would rather Sara Jane not know about it just yet." Levi knew it wouldn't do any good to argue with her about it. The Amish were accustomed to making the little ones' beds; they were excellent carpenters. He wanted to tell her this, but he didn't want to hurt her feelings.

Levi had practically torn down the barn and built it all over again. Several of the Amish men came over and helped rebuild. He had begun his own blacksmith shop in the barn and already had all the Amish men's business. Levi said to Sara Jane, "With a new baby coming, I wonder if I could get some of the town folks who have farms to come. I think I will ride into Ruby Hope this afternoon. I want to go talk with Mr. Troyer, who runs the hardware store and ask him if he could put the word out about my shop."

In Ruby Hope soon afterward, Levi stopped by the hardware store and spoke with the owner. The owner said. "I will do what I can, Levi. I'll let my customers know about your shop."

Two weeks went by before Levi saw a couple of men pull up in a pickup truck. They came to talk to him about the horses they had on their ranch. "I have a big ranch on the outskirts of town with about fifty horses, and I need a good blacksmith to take care of them," the driver of the truck said after they had introduced themselves. "I was wondering if you could come out and look at them." Levi replied to the gentlemen, "Yes, I would be glad to help you out. Just let me know when a good time would be to spend examining the horses. Do you have a list, with you?" The ranch owner did. Fifty horse's times four hooves were a lot of shoes. It would take at least a day to examine their hooves, meet the stable management, and assess their needs. Levi was happy to get some business from people in town. After the new customers left, he started thinking. "I might need to hire an extra man to help out around here. The business could start getting really busy."

Levi asked his brother Samuel if he would like to work with him in his shop.

Samuel had been helping a friend do some work on a farm, and he was glad of the prospect of more consistent work with family. He said. "I would love to work with you, Levi. I think it would be a great opportunity for me to learn the blacksmith trade." After Samuel and Levi began working together in the shop, the business did indeed grow. Levi felt particularly good about this arrangement because he knew he could leave Samuel there to handle things whenever he had to go out to a farm.

Chapter Fourteen

One afternoon, Levi left the shop to go out to one of the ranches. During the period of time he was gone, Samuel oversaw the shop. Levi had been gone for a couple of hours when

Samuel accidentally dropped the heated hammer head that scattered sparks all over the ground in the shop. The fire got bigger and bigger, and Samuel tried to put it out but was overcome from the smoke.

He ran out to the road and tried to find someone to help. Sara Jane was pregnant and couldn't do much. She ran out to the barn and grabbed a bucket. She filled the bucket full of water and started throwing it on the fire. But it became too much for her too. It wasn't long before several of the Amish neighbors saw the smoke and came to help.

After a long period, the fire was out. No more than half the barn had burned down so Levi would be able to salvage a few things. He had come home during which time the barn was in flames and began panicking when he saw the fire. His main concern was Sara Jane, so he ran to make sure she was ok. The men assured Levi that they would have his barn rebuilt in no time. They said. "We will be out here first thing in the morning, Levi. We'll get started rebuilding the shop and have it up and running before you know it." "Thanks for helping," he said honestly. "I will see all of you in the morning." He stood there just looking at his barn. Much of his equipment was lost.

Then he recollected himself. Or at least he tried. "I need to talk to Samuel and find out what happened." Samuel tried to explain that it was an accident, but Levi was too upset; he wouldn't let his brother tell his side of the story. Levi just stood there shaking his head with his straw hat in his hands. Afterwards, he said, "Samuel, you are reckless and immature, and I can't have someone like that working for me. You need to grow up. You put Sara Jane in danger.

When I pulled into the yard, I just knew something had happened to her and the baby." Samuel felt ashamed and hurt and knew that even though it was an accident, he was not going to convince Levi of that. So, he decided the best thing he could do was to get on his horse and leave. He knew there was no use in trying to talk to his older brother right then; he was just too upset.

The days that followed were hard for Levi. The Amish men in their community came out every day for several days to help him get his barn back up. They worked hard all day long each time, putting up new walls and a roof. The barn turned out to be better than it was before. It was more sturdy and modern. They cleaned up the floors and got his tools cleaned and ready to use. Levi was amazed and couldn't thank the men enough. "Thank you all for your help," he told them, and he promised "I will be there if you'll ever need my help."

She was growing bigger and bigger and beginning to have some problems getting around. Her feet were swollen, and she seemed to be very tired all the time. The midwife said to her, "Sara Jane, you need complete bed rest until time for the baby".

A few of the Amish women came to the farm and made dinner for them. One of her neighbors stayed with her to make sure she didn't try to get up. She needed to just rest and try to get her feet to return to their normal size. Levi was very concerned about her and was constantly looking in on her. Levi said, "Can I get you some water, Sara Jane? Let me pull the blankets up around you, I don't want you to get cold." He hovered until the midwife said to him,

"Go back to work, and I will let you know if anything should happen." So, Levi walked out to his barn and began working on a cradle he was making for the baby.

Chapter Fifteen

The next day Betty Anne came to visit and found Sara Jane in bed. She was worried about her and said. "You need a real doctor, Sara Jane." "I've told you before, the Amish women deliver the babies in the community; I will be just fine."

Betty Anne had a hard time with this, but she tried to understand. She asked the midwife,

"Is there anything I can do for her?" The midwife, Danielle, shook her head. She told Betty Anne, "Just go and sit with her for a spell, because there is nothing you can do right now."

Levi was building a cradle for the baby but figured she wanted to keep the modern baby bed that Betty Anne gave her. He started thinking out loud. "Maybe she could use the cradle in the kitchen while she is cooking or cleaning; then she could keep a close eye on him." He knew how close the two women were and didn't want to hurt anyone's feelings.

After Betty Anne went home, Levi brought the cradle in for her to see. She was touched that Levi had made the cradle and said to him, "I will use both the beds for the baby. I know you don't approve of the baby bed, but Betty Anne is like a Mother I never had; she gave us the baby bed with as much love as she would her own daughter." Betty Anne couldn't be expected to understand their Amish ways, and he tried to console himself with this fact. He knew how Sara Jane felt about her, so he pushed it out of his mind.

The baby was born on January 10, 1978 with the midwife attending. She had a hard time delivering the baby boy, whom they named Joseph Levi Click. "That is a great name for my little son." Replied Levi. Sara Jane said. "The baby looks frail to me, Levi; I'm having a hard time getting him to drink his milk. He isn't growing like he should either."

"I think as time goes by, he will start to come around, Sara Jane. He's just getting a slow start, that's all."

Betty Anne became concerned about the child as he began to run a fever from time to time. She had become close to her and didn't mind giving her advice. She said, "Sara Jane, you need to take Joseph Levi to a doctor. My past nursing experience tells me something bad is wrong with him. It's not normal for a child to run a fever as much as he does. I would be happy to take you and Joseph Levi to his appointment. Please think about it, Sara Jane."

He continued to run a fever off and on. Sara Jane worried about the child constantly.

In December 1981 she announced to Levi she was going to have another baby. Joseph Levi would be four years old in January the following year.

Sara Jane was carrying the second child without any problems. Levi said. "Sara Jane, I know you aren't far along with the second child, but I have decided to have a neighbor come two days a week; she can take care of the laundry and cook the meals for us." "I'm looking forward to the help, Levi, since Joseph Levi is almost four years old. It will be a big help to me."

When Joseph Levi turned four years old she wanted to have a big party to celebrate his birthday. It was 1982, and the weather was still cold and nasty. She invited a few folks to come to his birthday party. The women brought casseroles, pies, cakes, and fried chicken. The food filled the whole kitchen table and smelled delicious. Betty Anne came to help Sara Jane get Joseph Levi ready for his big day. He was so excited and running around singing "Happy Birthday to me." He was an adorable child, and Betty Anne thought the world of him; she loved him as if he were her own grandchild. She said. "It's a pleasure to be around all these wonderful people who care so much for one another." It had become common to see her always there; she was such a good friend to the young couple.

The following day, Sara Jane got in touch with Betty Anne. "Could you make an appointment for Joseph Levi to see a different doctor. He has been running a fever all night; I am so worried about him." She said. "Levi, Betty Anne is coming to pick us up and taking

Joseph Levi to see a doctor outside the Amish community." Levi was hesitant but decided that maybe it was for the best. Betty Anne made the appointment right away. She said. "Sara Jane, I will come and pick you up in the morning."

Chapter Sixteen

His little body seemed small as he lay in his mother's arms. Levi said, "Sara Jane, maybe he played too much at his party, running and playing with the other kids." "I know, Levi, but the fevers have happened too often; since he was born. I want to have a different doctor look at him, if simply to ease my mind." The following morning, Betty Anne came for Sara Jane and Joseph Levi in her car. While waiting to see the doctor, they talked a about the baby she was carrying. She knew she needed to get Sara Jane's mind off the sick child for a while.

At last, they were called in to the doctor's office; he examined Joseph Levi and took his temperature. His face had a look of concern on it. He said, "The boy is going to need to have some blood work before I can make a diagnosis." Betty Anne asked her to please give some thought to what the doctor said: "You must let the doctors draw blood, otherwise we may never find out what Joseph Levi's problems are." She knew that Levi would not approve of the test. She decided to go ahead and let them do the test without Levi's consent. She was very worried about the child and just wanted to find out what was wrong with him.

The nurses and the doctor took pains to be very calm and reassuring with Joseph Levi as his blood was drawn. He cried but was otherwise very brave. It just took a few minutes but seemed like a long time to his Mother. As she waited for the lab results, she prayed silently.

When they returned to his office, the doctor met her with a grave look on his face. He said, "Could you two ladies please sit down so we can talk? Joseph Levi seems to have some kidney problems and will need special help and medications." Betty Anne understood everything, but

Sara Jane was confused.

The doctor explained to them, very patiently, "The creatinine levels in his blood are unusually high, and he needs a specialist called a nephrologist. Elevated creatinine level signifies impaired kidney function or kidney disease. This is very dangerous for the child."

She was having a hard time understanding and started to cry. So, the doctor tried again to explain everything to her. He said, "Creatinine in the blood is generally normal, but the boys were around nine, and it means his kidneys are failing. You need to make an appointment with a nephrologist at once." Betty Anne asked the nurse to give her the number for a good nephrologist in the area. She called and set up an appointment for the child the following day.

The next morning, Betty Anne returned for Sara Jane and Joseph Levi in her car. They had an appointment at ten, and she didn't want them to be late. The nephrologist had received the report from the primary care doctor and knew about Joseph Levi's elevated creatinine levels. He said, "I am very concerned about the child. He needs to go into the hospital to have a shunt inserted into his arm. He will need to be put on a dialysis machine until he can get a new kidney.

The dialysis machine will function as a kidney to get rid of the waste in his kidneys."

Note: Nephrologist
A Nephrologist is a medical doctor who specializes in kidney care and treating diseases of the kidneys. End-Stage-Renal-Disease refers to a permanent condition in which the kidneys are no longer able to filter waste.

Note: Creatinine in the Blood
Elevated creatinine level signifies impaired kidney function or kidney disease. Abnormally high levels of creatinine thus warn of possible malfunction or failure of the kidneys. It is for this reason standard blood tests routinely check the amount of creatinine in the blood.

Note:
An Arteriovenous graft for his hemodialysis is created by connecting a vein to an artery using a soft plastic tube. After the graft has healed,

hemodialysis is performed by placing two needles; one in the arterial side and one in the venous side of the graft. The graft allows for increased blood flow. They call the shunt a fistula (Arteriovenous)

Joseph Levi had to have the shunt put into his arm to keep him alive until a kidney was found for him. Being as young as he was Betty Anne knew it was just a matter of time before they found a match.

Chapter Seventeen

It was very hard for Sara Jane. In addition to her worry about her child, she knew she must explain all this to Levi. She looked at Betty Anne and said. "I'm going to need your help explaining this. I'm going to have to go home and talk to Levi and see what he says." The doctor continued," The boy is very sick, and you shouldn't take too long. This is a life-threatening condition."

The two women braced for the worst. They knew what they had to tell him was going to be heartbreaking. She thought that Betty Anne should be the one to give him the details about the disease. She was still a little uncertain about it all. "Don't worry, Sara Jane," Betty Anne told her friend. "I will take care of everything."

She dropped Sara Jane and Joseph Levi off at the farm and said, "I will be back this evening to talk with Levi. Don't you worry now, everything is going to be alright."

She decided she would stop by the library and check out some books on kidney disease. She wanted to learn as much as she could about it before she spoke to Levi. Then maybe she could help her friends understand and get through this terrible ordeal. Her heart was breaking just thinking about what this little child had to go through at such a young age. She thought to herself, "most people are grown when they have to go through something as serious as this. I'm so glad the doctors found out as soon as they did about his kidneys." She said a silent prayer for the child as she drove down the dirt road leading to the farm.

When Betty Anne spoke to Levi, she was very direct. "Joseph Levi has a disease that is very serious. It's a life-threatening disease, and the absolute way to save his life is to follow the doctors' instructions. His kidneys are failing, and he is going to have to have a new kidney to survive. They will need to put a shunt in his arm, so they can perform dialysis on him until he receives a new kidney. Do you understand Levi? He was devastated and sank to the floor as he said a silent prayer: "God, why did this have to happen to my son, why God?" What can I do Betty Anne? How can I help my son?" "All we can do right now is pray and let the doctors take care of Joseph Levi."

That evening, she sat down with her friends and tried to explain everything to them. She wanted them to understand what the doctors were going to do to help their son. The shunt in his arm and the dialysis were confusing to them both; as she continued to explain as best she could.

They felt so grateful to their friend for explaining everything to them. No one in their Amish community had ever experienced this kind of disease before and it was hard for them understand.

But with Betty Anne's help and guidance they knew what they had to face now.

Note:

Once the kidney function goes below 10 -15 percent of normal, dialysis treatments or a kidney transplant is necessary to sustain life.

Chapter Eighteen

Levi went to see the Bishop to let him know about his son. He needed the clergyman to pray for Joseph Levi and to pray for him, to have the strength he needed to get through this. He lowered his head and sank to his knees as he cried. The Bishop put his hand on Levi's shoulder and prayed silently.

The Amish Community was in shock when they heard the news from the Bishop.

A neighbor, Jonathan Yoder said to the Bishop, "Our community would like to give the click family as much assistance as we can. We want to help them get through this with their little son."

The following morning Levi hitched the horse to the enclosed buggy and helped Sara Jane and Joseph Levi climb inside. It was freezing outside, and the wind blew so strongly they hardly saw where they were going. Betty Anne said. "I will meet you at the hospital." She knew Levi would not ride in a car, and she didn't want to upset him any more than he already was, specifically at a time like this. He had always been a strong man, but this had brought him to his knees; and he felt so helpless.

They arrived at the hospital, and the nurses urgently took the child to the operating room to prep him for minor surgery. The doctor explained to Levi, "He has to have a shunt put in his arm, so we can perform dialysis on him. His kidneys are small and not growing like they should; they're not filtering the waste out of his body."

The doctor also told the child's parents, "He needs to undergo certain tests. I suggest that he stays in the hospital. In my opinion, Joseph Levi is too small and frail to go home ' right now. You would need to take him to the clinic at least three or four times a week for his dialysis." The two of them just couldn't understand the position the child was in.

The doctor sat down with them and tried to explain the situation. He hoped to make them understand the seriousness of it. "The boy should not go home right now; you are just not equipped to take care of him as he should be." Determinately, Betty Anne convinced them that the doctor was right. She said. "Sara Jane, you and Levi can come every day to see him and stay if you want to. Joseph Levi will be better off staying in the hospital. It would be best for you, too, Sara Jane. You need to take care of yourself as well."

Levi drove the buggy home and met with the Bishop again. He tried to explain his son's kidney failure and said he needed a new kidney. He said, "What should I do?"

The Bishop said. "Levi, please pray with me to see if we can find the answer to your problem."

After the word got out about Joseph Levi, the Amish community started bringing food to their home and doing chores for the family.

He prayed for the answer to his problem. Ultimately, the answer came to him. "I should be the one to give my son a kidney. I'm his father, and I don't want someone else's organ in my child."

Note: Transplantation in children that necessitate specialized approaches and have resulted in clinical advances so that kidney transplantation in young children have higher success rates than in any other age group

A Poem Written by Sabrina A. Hernandez

"My little boy"

No amount of gold could ever compare to the gift of love my son shares.
I've been blind, and I couldn't see that all the love I've wanted is right here in front of me.
He gives me reason to get through another day
Maybe it's how he loves me in his special little way.
And when it gets hard for me to sleep at night…
He wraps his little arms around me and says God will make things right!
From sweet gentle touches to his bear hugs and a kiss…
He makes this hell on earth seem more like a peaceful bliss.
That great big Kool-Aid smile and the twinkle in his eyes…
Every time I look at him it makes me want to cry.
But they're not tears of sorrow; they're tears of pride and joy…
To know that all the love in heaven is wrapped around my little boy…

Chapter Nineteen

He decided to talk to Sara Jane about this as soon as possible. He said, "I can't stand the thought of our boy lying in the hospital sick without us being able to do anything for him. I want to give him one of my kidneys. I have prayed and prayed and decided that is what I want to do."

She didn't know what to think. She was so worried about the child, and now Levi wanted to put his life at risk. She wanted to speak with Betty Anne about it. She trusted her and knew she would know what to do.

Betty Anne felt much more positive in response to this idea than she had. She knew that Levi would be the perfect candidate. She told her friend, "I advise you and Levi to go ahead and speak with the doctor about this."

The days that followed were critical for the child as Levi struggled with his decision. But he decided to go ahead and talk to the doctor as Betty Anne had advised him to do. The doctor said, "Mr. Click, that is one of the most thoughtful and loving things a father can do for his son. I think it's a wonderful idea to donate your kidney to Joseph Levi. You will need to be tested first to make sure the two of you are a compatible match." Levi consented to take the test, and he turned out to be a perfect match for the child. Everyone was happy for them and knew this was the right decision to make.

The day came for the surgery, and the waiting rooms were filled with friends. So many horses and buggies occupied the parking area that hardly anyone was able to park their cars. The nurses and doctors had never seen so many Amish people in one area. The hospital staff helped to make them feel comfortable while there. This was a special day for this little boy, and now he would have a chance at a healthy life.

The surgery was a success for the child and his father. Sara Jane and Betty Anne had a hard time looking at Joseph Levi in so much pain the morning after surgery. His little face was white as a sheet as he said, "Mommy, I hurt, Mommy, I hurt. The two women broke down and cried without any shame. They hugged each other and tried to hide their tears from the child. The 'following morning, he was wide awake, and the nurses had him sitting up in bed. His cheeks were rosy, and the nurse said, "this little fellow is hungry. He's going to be just fine."

The days and months that followed were happy ones for the Click family. Levi was mending well after his surgery. Joseph Levi had a good appetite and was putting on weight. His cheeks were still rosy, and he played like a normal boy. The Amish community continued to help Levi on his farm. The women brought over all sorts of casseroles, cakes, and pies. The people in the Valley also continued to come out to the Amish community and offer their help. They were all so concerned and wanted to do something for them. Betty Anne knew that the people in her town were generous folks, and once again they would be willing to pitch in and help with the expenses they had encountered. All their prayers had been answered, and their lives would continually be changed for the better.

The Amish men and women had helped the Clicks all summer, getting through their hard times. In August the time came for her to give birth to her second child. Her pregnancy had been much better than the first, and she decided the midwife can help her again when the time comes.

Betty Anne knew she was due anytime, even though the Amish don't keep a calendar or calculate when the baby is due, they just know. Betty Anne told her, "Sara Jane, I want to be here when the baby is born, but I'm working full time now in the flower shop. I miss seeing you and Joseph Levi. I'll try to get back out here as soon as I can. My schedule is full right now. I have Sundays off, so I'll come back out to see you then." Another week went by, then Betty Anne decided to ride out to the country.

When she arrived, the midwife was there, and Betty Anne knew it must be time for the baby. She was so happy she had chosen to go that day. Samuel John arrived without any complications and was a healthy baby. Two boys, she thought. She is going to have her hands full. She did so well with baby number two that she was up and around the house, cooking and cleaning, in no time. She seemed to adapt to her regular routine and felt much better. She was in a happy place now that Joseph Levi and his father were still doing well and the new baby was healthy.

Chapter Twenty

The town started decorating for the fall season. September and October were beautiful months, with all the fall colors of yellow, gold, and red. The store fronts were once again decorated for the season, and the kids that walked by just had to have a pumpkin. The Amish porches were decorated with pumpkins, and the fields were bright with the colors of fall.

Sara Jane had decorated her front porch with all sizes of pumpkins, and the house smelled of pumpkin and apple pie. She mused to herself. "The aroma of the pumpkin and apple pies make me think of my mother. She was always baking pies and cakes; and I loved licking the bowls. Those scents bring back so many wonderful memories of my childhood."

November began to grow colder and colder as the Amish people started getting ready for the Thanksgiving holidays. She always had a feast of turkey, potatoes, stuffing, and, of course, pumpkin pie. She also baked Betty Anne's favorite apple pie, along with pecan and egg custard. She loved this time of the year and felt they had so much to be thankful for this holiday season. She was grateful Levi and Joseph Levi's health was good, and for little Samuel John. She invited Betty Anne, her father, John, Grandmother and Grandpa to come and enjoy their feast. This was a Thanksgiving they would always remember.

Betty Anne loved going out to visit them on their farm, and she always brought Joseph Levi a small toy. She had come to feel as if he were her own grandson, and Sara Jane was her daughter. She wanted to always be there for them. She started thinking about her own kids, and she wondered, aloud as she drove around town one day: "Will I ever hear from my children again?"

Levi had become accustomed to Betty Anne, and he counted her among his blessings.

He thought to himself over the holiday, "I feel so much gratitude toward her. If it had not been for her encouraging us to take Joseph Levi to see an outside doctor, the boy may have died."

The town of Ruby Hope got a lot of snow during the winter months, and the roads were always treacherous and hard to drive on. Levi always kept lots of wood chopped and stacked on the back porch. The white house was consistently warm from the wood burning in the big fireplace.

Since the new baby's arrival, Samuel had wanted to come out to the farm and try to make amends with Levi about the barn fire. He knew Levi had been through a lot over the past few months, and he was worried about what to say to him. He said to himself, "I can at least explain my side of the story and tell him I'm sorry." The whole thing had plagued him ever since. He rode his horse even though the weather was cold.

Christmas was approaching once again, and the year was 1982. Ruby Hope was abuzz with holiday excitement. Samuel had started coming out to the farm to visit with the family. He wanted to make it up to Levi somehow and had missed being with his brother.

He brought presents for Joseph Levi and was always helping Sara Jane with her chores.

Betty Anne was once again stuck in the house because of the bad weather. She knew the roads were bad, and she shouldn't be driving. Still, she longed to be with Sara Jane, Joseph Levi, and the new baby, since Christmas was simply a week away. At long last, two days before Christmas the snow stopped, and the weather began to clear. The roads were still scattered with debris and fallen tree limbs. She drove into town and did her shopping. She wanted to see how bad the roads really were.

Despite of the bad weather, she made up her mind to go to the farm for Christmas.

Samuel also decided to go spend Christmas with Levi and his family. He hitched his buggy to his horse and started toward the farm. She had been trying to bake all morning, but the baby wouldn't stop crying. Just as Betty Anne said, she had her hands full. She thought to herself,

"where is Betty Anne when I need her?"

As she made her way out to the farm she started to reminisce about Danny and Sadie and how they always looked forth to Christmas. Thinking out loud, she said, "I remember making fudge and cookies and putting them in a tin box under the Christmas tree. Santa gave Sadie a small baby doll and Danny a baseball bat and ball. Oh, how I miss those days; wonder where they are now? I wish I could at least hear from them." She continued to reminisce about the past as she drove. "It's like they left and never looked back. When John died, I had to work to support them. I don't know what I should have done differently. I wouldn't have been able to give them anything at all if I hadn't worked those long hours." Tears began to fall down her face until she barely saw the road to drive. She began to talk to herself again. "I'm so lucky to have Sara Jane in my life. God knew I needed somebody; so, he sent me her." She said a silent prayer for Sadie and Danny, and thanked God for sending her Sara Jane.

Chapter Twenty-One

As she was driving down the dirt roads leading to the farm, the trees glistened with snow, and she saw several deer crossing the roads. It was a beautiful sight and made her feel happy to be alive. When she arrived, she saw Samuel's buggy in the driveway. She thought how wonderful it was that he had made up with his brother and now they can spend Christmas together. Sara Jane was happy to see Betty Anne, and welcomed her inside, telling her," Grandmother Ruth, Grandpa Abram, Dad and John are coming out Christmas morning."

She seemed so content to have all her family coming for Christmas.

She had been baking all day and had a nice dinner made for all of them. She said, "Betty Anne, I am so happy you decided to spend Christmas Eve with us." They hugged as she said, "I love you just like you were my own Mother." Betty Anne started to cry. "that means so much to me. For several years I have spent Christmas by oneself, and it feels so good to be with people I care about."

The following morning, Sara Jane got up early and started the fire going in the fireplace. She walked into the kitchen and started up the wood burning stove, lit all the lanterns, and proceeded to make breakfast. She prepared pancakes, sausage, biscuits, and gravy for the family. She knew they would be coming soon, so she wanted to get things cooked as soon as possible. Joseph Levi had already woken up and started down the steps. When She heard him coming, she started getting his medications crushed up, so she could put them in his oatmeal.

Even though he was almost five now, that was the one way she got him to take his medicine.

Note:
Immunosuppressant's are drugs or medicines that lower the body's ability

to reject a Transplanted organ. Another term for these drugs is anti-rejection drugs.

It wasn't long before Betty Anne and Samuel came into the kitchen to help. He set the table and asked, "Is there anything else I can help you with?" She gestured toward a chair. "I have a hot pot of tea ready for you'll, sit down and drink your tea. I have breakfast almost ready. Levi has been up since five this morning. He is out in the barn taking care of the animals."

They had a few chickens, a cow, and a horse. Levi knew it was going to be a busy day for the family, so he wanted to make sure the animals were taken care of early. She had already started cooking the sausage. After she had a hearty breakfast ready for everyone, she saw Dad's horse and buggy pull into the driveway. She said, "Well, they are just in time".

They all sat down to a nice breakfast, and Dad said the silent prayer.

Betty Anne realized the Amish don't celebrate Christmas with Christmas trees.

However, they do love to send and receive Christmas cards. The family had received several cards during the holiday season. Sara Jane hung them around the house as decorations. She baked blueberry, apple, and pumpkin pies to celebrate the holidays, and the house always smelled wonderful. Betty Anne felt like she was at home. She loved the simple ways of the Amish people and enjoyed being with them during the holidays.

After Christmas the snow and ice began to thaw, making the roads somewhat easier for the horses to trot on. Spring was on the way, and the young men and women of the Amish community had begun to court. John and Samuel were at the age of courting and started going to the singings on Sunday evenings. Samuel met a girl by the name of Mattie Sue. He would take her home in his buggy every Sunday evening after the singings. John, on the other hand, had met two girls he liked and couldn't decide which one he liked the best. Wanda and Henrietta were both nice girls, and if anything, this made John's decision more difficult.

Note:

Pennsylvania German pronunciation (ram springe) is a term for a rite of passage during adolescence, translated in English as "jumping/hopping around," used in some Amish and Mennonite communities.

Samuel had started working with his brother again in the blacksmith shop and didn't have a lot of time for dating. He liked Mattie Sue and thought he might ask her to go driving around with him one Sunday afternoon. He would get to know her better if he was able to spend more time with her. At the next Sunday night singing he said, "Mattie Sue, would you like to go driving around with me next Sunday?"

Mattie Sue was delighted. She said, "Yes, Samuel, I would love to go riding around with you." Sara Jane knew Mattie Sue's family. She told Samuel, "She comes from a large family and is the last one of the girls to get married. Did you know she has four sisters?" Mattie Sue liked Samuel and had heard of Levi and Sara Jane. Sometimes she would see them at Market or in the town of Ruby Hope. She always spoke to them when she passed them. Sara Jane knew just about all the people that lived in their community, but some of the younger girls and boys were not as well-known as their fathers and mothers were.

Chapter Twenty-Two

One day when they worked together in the smithy, Samuel impulsively said, "Levi, I have a lot of feelings for Mattie Sue, and I am thinking about getting engaged." Levi was very surprised to hear this. He told his brother, "I'm happy for you, but I wouldn't rush into anything. Both of you need to get baptized first before making any plans." Samuel decided he would court Mattie Sue for a while longer and see if this truly was the right girl for him.

Levi was thinking about changes also. He had started talking about buying a farm that had a bigger house. He mentioned this to his wife one evening after dinner. "Sara Jane, one of your Dad's neighbor has decided to move and sell their farm. They want to move to Lancaster County. The parcel has about seventy-five acres and a big barn with a nice two-story house. It's located on a hill overlooking the farm land. You can sit on the front porch and look out over the land. There are three bedrooms upstairs, and the large kitchen has a screened in porch attached to the back of the house. The kitchen is equipped with loads of cabinets and a big stove." It was a wood burning stove, of course, as no one in the Amish community had electricity. Levi continued, "The sitting room has a huge fireplace and lots of room for family and company."

Sara Jane said, "It sounds wonderful, and I am very happy that it is near my family.

I will be able to visit my Grandparents whenever I want to; they love seeing the children when they can." For his part, Levi was excited about the farm and the barn. He would expand his blacksmith business and have the land to plant corn, beans, and pumpkins on. He said, "When we get settled in the new house I'm going to buy a few more farm animals. We'll have plenty of room for them there."

After having this conversation and beginning their plans for a move, she decided to take a walk around their old place and ponder everything that had happened in her life over the past year. She loved Levi and knew he would do what was best for his family. She walked all around the property and stood and gazed at their field. She remembered when he first brought her here to show her the place before they married. She had been happy here except for Joseph Levi's kidney failure. She didn't want to think about all that, but it weighed heavy on her mind. It was something she would never forget. She said a silent prayer thanking God for all her blessings.

The sale went through without a hitch; the neighbor had been relieved to be able to sell so quick. Ultimately, the day came when Levi closed on the farm, and it was time to move. The whole Amish community came out to help pack and load up the buggies. The women brought and all kinds of cakes and cookies for the kids. She had already packed the kids' toys and clothes and was ready to sit down for a bit. The older Amish girls were looking after Joseph Levi and Samuel John, so she would be able to relax for a moment.

Without warning, Betty Anne came driving up in her car, jumped out, and said, "Here I am, where should I start packing?" Sara Jane was so happy to see her that she ran and put her arms around her and said, "Thank you for coming, I don't know what I would do without you! "You know I wouldn't miss your moving day for the world. I am happy to help. Now, let's put some of those boxes in the trunk of my car."

The Amish folks were used to Betty Anne and her outside ways, and they liked her and knew she was a good Christian woman. They don't normally allow cars on their property, but in Betty Anne's case nobody minded at all. She was a true trusted friend of the Amish community.

The new farm wasn't as big as some of the other farms, but it was big enough for them. Sara Jane found a beautiful spot along the side of the house where she intended to plant flowers. She could hardly wait to get started with the planting. The barn was big and had plenty of room for the animals and Levi's blacksmith shop. He was hoping to get more business, and now he had his brother to help him. "Samuel, I'm going to teach you the right ways to handle a hammer and all the things you need to know about being a blacksmith". Samuel was also good with animals, and Levi knew he would be able to count on his brother to help him.

Chapter Twenty-Three

As summer was ending Sara Jane and Levi were still settling into the farm.

She was trying to unpack and get the kitchen in order. She wanted to start baking cakes and pies again and couldn't wait to get started. Samuel John had started walking and was into everything, so Joseph Levi would look after the baby for her. He was such a big help to Sara

Jane. She would bake them oatmeal cookies and spoil them both. Joseph Levi was five now, and his health was mending well. She was so proud of her two little boys.

Betty Anne thought of the two boys as her own grandchildren, and every time she came out to the farm, she would bring them a small gift. Levi wasn't very happy about all the gifts. He said, "Sara Jane, Betty Anne is spoiling our kids. You need to tell her to stop giving them things; it isn't our way." Joseph Levi and Samuel John have more toys than any other child in the community."

Sara Jane thought it was sweet of Betty Anne but decided to have a talk with her about the gifts. She knew Levi was not happy about it and she didn't want any hard feelings between them. The next time Betty Anne came out she brought the boys a small gift as usual. Sara Jane decided she would speak to her about it then. She said, "We truly appreciate what you do for the kids, Betty Anne, but it isn't our way. We don't give gifts except maybe on special occasions. We would rather you just come and visit with the boys." Joseph Levi and the baby loved Betty Anne and got excited when they saw her car pull into the yard.

Betty Anne tried to understand. She didn't want to cause any trouble between the couple, so she decided she would simply bring them a small gift occasionally. She felt hurt, but she loved this family so much that she decided she would do as she asked. As Sara Jane and Levi settled into their new home, they were at last able to relax. She had gotten the kitchen in order, so she started baking as usual, and she was so thankful to be close to her family once again.

Fall returned to Ruby Hope, and the leaves on the trees had started to turn. The year was 1983, and the big oak trees that lined Main Street were filled with beautiful medleys of golden brown, red, and yellow leaves. They shimmered like gemstones when the sun shone on them. The farm fields were full of all kinds of pumpkins. All the farmers in the area were loading them up into big trucks and taking them to market.

Decorations of fall colors were seen all over the county, on porches, in store windows and along the sidewalks of the town. Ruby Hope Valley, Pennsylvania was such a lovely town. Betty Anne was happy to be a part of it as well as the Amish Community. The Amish people had bails of straw lined down the fences of their driveways as well as pumpkins. It was a beautiful sight to see as she made her way through the countryside. Every time she drove out to the Amish Community she was in awe of all the lovely farms and the land surrounding them. It looked like a picture post card. She felt so honored to be called a friend of all the people there.

Chapter Twenty-Four

Betty Anne didn't get to go see Sara Jane and the kids as often as she wished because of her full-time job at the hospital flower shop. She had not been feeling very well in recent times and didn't often have the strength to drive the long distance. She thought to herself, "I think I will make an appointment with my doctor for a checkup. I don't seem to have the energy I used to."

Not seeing her friend as often, she began to worry about Betty Anne. She mused to herself as she kneaded some bread one morning: "I wonder why I haven't seen or heard from her. It's not like her to stay away from us so long." The nearest phone booth was in a field along the road which led to Mark's farm, so she decided to walk down there and call her friend. But no one was home.

Betty Anne had gone to the doctor for a checkup. The doctor had a grave look on his face when he returned with her report. He told her, "Betty Anne, your blood pressure is way too high, and you have been losing weight rapidly. This concerns me. I want you to go take some tests, so we can rule out some things."

When she got home, she found she had gotten a call from Sara Jane and was sorry she missed it. She knew she couldn't call her back, so she hoped she would call again. She decided to lie down for a bit and slipped off to sleep; she felt so tired today for some reason.

The next morning the nurse from the doctor's office called to set up an appointment for her to have some tests. She had an EKG, a chest x-ray, and a stress test. She was exhausted after all that. The nurse set up an appointment to go over her test results the following week.

When Betty Anne went in for her appointment to get the test results, Doctor Lane said, "You have a heart valve condition. Your heart is very weak, and that was why you have been getting so tired." He started her on a heart medication and warned her not to be lifting anything heavy. She was surprised at these results because she had never had these kinds of problems with her heart before. Betty Anne was always worrying about her two kids. She felt a lot of anxiety and uncertainty. She wondered if this had weakened her heart over the years.

In any case, she decided she would keep this to herself for the time being; she didn't want to alarm Sara Jane. When she felt better she would take a ride out to the farm to see the kids.

Levi and Sara Jane were very concerned for their friend and prayed for her every day. She said, "Levi, as soon as I can, I want to go into town to see Betty Anne. I worry that maybe she has a health problem we need to know about? After all, I am like a daughter to her, and I should know what's going on."

Another week rolled by, and Betty Anne's condition began to worsen; her strength started to fade, and she barely made it to work every day. Doctor Lane, when she went back, informed her that her heart condition had gotten worse, and that was causing her to feel so tired. She had always been kind of a private person and kept things in rather than talk about them. Just like the secret she carried around in her heart; Sara Jane was the sole person she had ever spoken to about that.

One afternoon Sara Jane got one of the Amish girls to come stay with the children whilst she took a trip into town. Levi hitched up the horse and buggy for her and helped her climb inside. When she arrived at Betty Anne's house, she found her friend lying down resting. Betty Anne was surprised to see her. She invited her in and they sat down at the kitchen table. Sara Jane said, "We have been worried about you and missed you coming to the farm." Betty dissembled. "I've been sick with a cold, and I didn't want to be around the kids until I got well. I've also been working six days a week at the flower shop.

Sundays are my single days off."

Sara Jane peered at her friend's face. "You are so pale! We have been concerned about your health. You need to eat some soup if you've had a cold!" She visited for a while longer, then decided it was getting late so she had better get started home. They hugged and said goodbye. As she climbed up into the buggy and started home, her mind was full of questions about Betty Anne as she guided the horse; all she could hear was the clip clopping of the horse's hoofs along the dirt road.

Betty Anne knew she had to do something to get her energy back, so she decided to talk to her doctor again. He might prescribe some good vitamins for her. When she got through to him, calling from the flower shop the next day, the doctor said, "I suggest a supplement of vitamins and minerals. Also, you should start walking some each day to try to get your strength back." This seemed reasonable to Betty. "I don't want to give up, doctor, so I'll do whatever you suggest getting better." A couple of weeks went by, still, before Betty Anne started to feel better.

She walked two miles a day after work, and she gradually began to get her strength back.

Chapter Twenty-Five

Winter was once again upon them, and she knew the weather was going to start getting worse, so she decided to take a trip out to the farm. The two boys were playing in the sitting room and heard the car when it pulled into the driveway; they became loud and excited when they saw Betty Anne drive up. She put the tea kettle on the wood burning stove and ran to the front door to greet her. She threw her arms around Betty Anne as tears begin to roll down her face. "I tried to force back the tears, but it was no use. I am so happy to see you. Levi and I have been so worried about you." They visited during the time they sat in the kitchen and drank tea. She had been baking again that morning, this time a casserole, and the aroma was so delightful along with the warmth from the wood burning stove; Betty Anne thought she might never go home again.

After she arrived home, the snow began to fall in Ruby Hope Valley. The window panes were so frosted you couldn't see outside. The roads and streets became impassable, so, as she had predicted, Betty Anne was once again stuck at home. Sara Jane just lived down the road from Mark's farm. She often took the children in the carriage to see her father. The Grandparents loved to see the two boys, too. The weather became too cold to take the boys out even for short trips like this. She felt bad about not being able to visit her Grandparents but knew they would understand. Her oldest brother, Caleb, and his family had moved into the big house with Mark and her brother John. Their three youngsters were Jenny, Rebecca, and Timothy. Maggie, Caleb's wife, loved to quilt, so Sara Jane and Maggie got along well.

Maggie had started having the quilting group at her house, so she would go down to the old home place and join in on the quilting. She had decided to make a quilt for Betty Anne.

The other women in the group said they would love to help her. She explained to them she wanted to finish the quilt by Christmas, because she needed to give it to her friend. It was going to be a beautiful quilt, with lots of pretty colors in it, such as deep red, purple, and dark green.

She knew she would love the quilt, and it could be a reminder of all her Amish friends.

Sara Jane and the other women finished the quilt just a week before Christmas.

It turned out beautifully, and she was thankful to the other women for helping her.

She knew they all liked and respected Betty Anne and thought the quilt was an excellent idea.

Christmas was just a week away, and she had invited Betty Anne to come and spend Christmas with them. Betty Anne was excited to be with the family during the holidays once again.

More people would be invited this year to Sara Jane and Levi's house, so they decided to set up a long table in the sitting room. The fire from the fireplace would keep everyone warm. She had invited her grandparents, Dad, and John, along with Caleb and his family. Samuel and Betty Anne were invited to come also. As the day approached, everyone was concerned about the weather. Levi said to his wife, "Betty Anne might have a problem getting out here this year. The weather is bad and doesn't look much like it's going to let up." Sara Jane was concerned about her and prayed the weather would get better.

She didn't want Betty Anne to have an accident.

She had been baking all week and the house smelled of apple, blueberry, and cherry pies.

The aroma from the kitchen was inviting as always. Maggie had been baking too and brought a macaroni and cheese casserole, pot roast with carrots and potatoes, a spice cake, and oatmeal cookies. The table was covered with all kinds of delicious dishes. Betty Anne was anxious to get there.

Note:

Nearly all Amish homes have a sizable garden, tended by the woman of the home with help from her children. Sweet corn, celery, beets, carrots, potatoes, tomatoes, peas, and a wide variety of other vegetables.

She knew the roads were bad, but she was determined to go to Sara Jane's house. She drove moderately and was very careful. It took her longer to get there, but she didn't care as long as she got there. After everyone arrived, they all sat down, and Mark said the silent prayer. Betty Anne couldn't have felt more at home.

Chapter Twenty-Six

After everyone else had gone home for the day, she gave Betty Anne the quilt. Her eyes began to tear up, and she threw her arms around her. They hugged each other for a long time. Then suddenly Joseph Levi and Samuel John came running up and put their arms around them. Betty Anne said, "I feel so truly blessed. This has been the most perfect Christmas, I have ever had."

Driving home, the roads were icy, and Betty Anne was afraid her car was going to slide off the road. As she came into a turn in the road, despite her best efforts to control it, her car slid right into a tree. She bumped her head on the steering wheel and passed out. An Amish gentleman came by driving his horse and buggy and saw the car up against the tree. He got out and saw Betty Anne inside the car; tried to get the door open, but it seemed be stuck. Not sure ' what to do next, he decided to get back in his buggy and go for help. He drove to the nearest farm and brought back Jacob and Jonathan Yoder to help him. The boys were strong and were able to pry the door open. As they pulled Betty Anne out of the car, they saw that she had blood all over her head and was unconscious. The men didn't know what to do, so the older gentlemen said, "Put her in your buggy and take her back to the Click's farm. They will know what to do and take care of her."

Betty Anne had just gone a little way down the road from the farm when she hit the tree, so the young men didn't have far to take her. Levi was coming out of the barn when he saw the buggy drive in from the road. He was surprised to see Jonathan and Jacob Yoder in the buggy. Jonathan Yoder said, "Levi, we have a lady friend of yours with us. She had an accident with her car and hit her head. Her car seems to have skidded off the road and hit a tree." Levi was shocked to see Betty Anne in the buggy. He said, "Boys, take her into the house." When Sara Jane saw them bringing Betty Anne in the house, she ran to help them and asked them to take her upstairs to the first bedroom. She was so scared and said to her husband, "You need to go to the phone booth and call the doctor, Levi."

When the doctor arrived, he went directly upstairs to see Betty Anne. She had a big bump on her head but otherwise seemed to be ok. He listened to her heart and checked her pulse.

The impact had broken the skin a little, but not badly enough to need stitches. He put a butterfly bandage on to hold the two sides together after he cleaned it. Feeling the antiseptic sting, Betty Anne opened her eyes. She had started to come around when she realized she was in Sara Jane's house. She asked her friend, what happened?" Sara Jane said, "Your car skidded off the road and hit a tree. You hit your head, and the boys down the road brought you here." She made a cup of hot tea, adding extra sugar, and brought her a plate of cookies. She fluffed the pillow up and told Betty Anne she was going to stay the night, so they can keep a close watch on her.

Betty Anne didn't feel like going home anyway; she was happy to be with these people that she cared so much about.

Before the doctor left he called Levi over to the door and said, "I'm worried about this woman. Her head seems alright, but her heart doesn't sound right. It sounds weak and you should keep a close watch on her. Call me if she isn't any better in the morning." Levi didn't understand what the doctor was trying to say to him and decided not to say anything to Sara Jane. She was already worried enough about her friend.

The following morning, she looked in on Betty Anne and noticed she was still sleeping, so she crept downstairs to the kitchen. She started the wood burning stove and lit all the lanterns. She walked into the sitting room and built a big fire in the fireplace. She wanted the house to be warm when Betty Anne and the children got up.

Levi had been in the barn since before daylight and wouldn't come in until breakfast. He fed all the animals and got his forge and fire pit started for the day. His brother would be coming over to the farm soon and he wanted everything to be ready.

Chapter Twenty-Seven

It was an exceptionally cold day, with snow and ice still on the ground. Debris from the trees were scattered all over the yard. The cold winter weather didn't look like it was going to let up anytime soon. She had started cooking breakfast when Betty Anne came down to the kitchen.

Sara Jane said. "I'm making pancakes for you." "Oh, please don't go to any trouble for me, Sara

Jane. Anything is fine with me." It might be a day or so before she can go home. She said, "Sara Jane would you mind calling my neighbor, Barbara, and letting her know what happened?" She said of course she wouldn't. She promised, "I'll run down to the phone booth, after breakfast and give her a call." Betty Anne said, "I actually hate to ask you to go out in this cold weather to use the phone." "No, I don't mind at all, replied Sara Jane.

The wood burning stove made the kitchen warm and the aroma of the food smelled delicious. "Can I help you do anything?" The older woman felt funny about her situation. "No, just sit down and enjoy a cool glass of milk. Or would you rather have a cup of hot tea?" "Hot tea sounds wonderful this morning."

Before long Levi and Samuel came in the back door. They took off their boots hung hats and coats up before coming into the kitchen. Their boots were covered in mud and made a mess on the porch floor. They both washed up in the kitchen sink and sat down at the kitchen table. Levi asked, "How are you feeling this morning, Betty Anne?" "I feel a lot better, thank you, Levi. I thought I would try to go home today. Do you think you might take me in your buggy? I plan to call the repair shop to come and pick up my car after I get home."

Levi glanced at Sara Jane. "I don't mind taking you, but the roads are still bad. I'm not sure, the horses can make it through all the snow."

"Ok, maybe Sara Jane can call the repair shop when she goes to call my neighbor, Barbara. I want to see if they can come and pick my car up."

The man at the shop, when they got through to him, said, "Our staff is used to this kind of weather. We will get out there today." Sara Jane said. "Betty Anne you look tired, why don't you lie down for a while?" She took her advice and walked back upstairs; she was feeling weak and tired.

As she dozed off, Betty Anne begin to dream about Danny and Sadie; it had become a habit of hers of late. She had been at Sara Jane's a couple of days now, and the weather looked like it was letting up some. Levi said, "I think the horses might be able to go through the mud since the snow and ice are melting away." She said her goodbyes and thanked them again for all they did for her, and the beautiful quilt she had made for her. She couldn't wait to show

Barbara. Levi helped Betty Anne into the buggy. It was an awfully cold day, so he asked her to wrap herself in the blankets. Picking up the reins, he signaled for the horses to go. The horses hesitated for a moment and then began to trot up the muddy road.

After arriving home, Betty Anne took a deep breath and thanked Levi again for taking care of her. She felt so blessed to have such wonderful friends and didn't know how she would ever repay their kindness. The past several years with this family had given her more faith and hope in her life; and she knew somehow that one day she was going to see her son and daughter again. Her neighbor Barbara came out to meet her and helped her out of the buggy and thanked Levi for bringing her home; he nodded and proceeded up the street.

Betty Anne was happy to see her neighbor and her dog Chloe and Boots the cat.

They sat for a while over a cup of coffee, at the same time she told Barbara about Christmas at Sara Jane's. She showed her the beautiful quilt that she had made for her. Barbara said, "The quilt is so lovely; you should be proud to have such wonderful friends in your life."

Betty Anne said, "Barbara, the Amish people taught me so many good things. I hope Sara Jane and I will always be friends. I have learned patience faith, hope, and love from these people. Being plain and simple is a good thing, Barbara. They don't need all the fancy things that most people have. We have our hair done at the beauty shop. We wear makeup and go to shops to buy our clothes. These people make their own clothes and never wear makeup."

Barbara nodded. "Betty Anne, you are lucky to know these people like you do. You know Amish people are misunderstood sometimes. When they come to town, people stare at them, particularly the young kids. I will never stare at them again; I know they are fine people. They have been so good to my best friend and neighbor." "I have also learned patience and kindness like I have never known before," Betty Anne added. "They truly do have big hearts and even though they are private people, they let me in their homes.

Barbara, next time I ride out to the farm, why don't you go with me? The landscape is beautiful and it's an enjoyable ride. I seem to reminisce a lot when I drive out there. It's just so peaceful and quiet I can't help thinking about Sadie and Danny and wondering what they are doing." "You know Betty Anne, you were a good Mother. It's not your fault those kids up and left you alone. You have got to stop blaming yourself and get on with your life. One day they may come walking in the door. You never know what God can do. He surprises me every day of my life."

Chapter Twenty-Eight

Winter began to fade as spring of 1986 brought beautiful colorful flowers. Everywhere you looked, yellow, pink, and orange flowers were popping up out of the ground. Sara Jane began to plant her flower garden. She planted lilies, daffodils, roses, petunias, and daisies. She said, "Levi, I want the prettiest flower garden I have ever had. I'm also thinking about planting blueberries along the side of the house. Would you help me?" "Of course, when do you want to get started planting?" Levi had put up a swing for the kids in the backyard to play on. This would give her time to tend to her garden without the kids bothering her. She was glad to see the cold wet weather go away. This would be the first summer at their new home, and she couldn't wait to sit on her big front porch and look at over the land.

Levi and Samuel's blacksmith business were doing well. They had customers coming from all over the county and the town of Ruby Hope Valley. Levi had purchased two more cows, a few pigs, several more chickens and two more horses. This way he could change the team out when he needed them to pull the buggy. He didn't like using the same horses all the time.

The weather was improving every day, and the fields had started to turn green. Levi and his brother took time from their job and decided to plow up the fields for planting. He wanted to plant corn, beans, and pumpkins. Most of the other Amish farmers planted pumpkins so they could sell them at market in the fall. It was too early to plant pumpkins, though, as he said to Samuel. "We'll get the pumpkins seeds in the ground in May.

By fall they should be ready to take to the market." She was so happy Levi decided to plant the pumpkins and imagined how beautiful the fields would be.

Joseph Levi was seven now and had started school. She realized he loved reading books about animals. He would read the Bible too and knew all the Bible verses the Bishop talked about in church. He read books over and over. By the time he started attending school he could read better than anyone in his class. She had been teaching him to read since he was just two. Amish children just get an eighth-grade education, and then the boys are expected to work the farm with their fathers. The girls are expected to keep house, bake, sew, and quilt.

Joseph Levi was already helping his Dad and Uncle Samuel in the barn occasionally. He was learning the blacksmith trade at an early age and knew how to feed the animals and do chores around the farm. He was proud of his son and knew they shared a special bond. Joseph Levi had few health problems since his kidney transplant, but Levi didn't want him overdoing it around the farm. He would caution his son from time to time to stop and rest, but the boy loved doing things and had so much energy that he couldn't slow down.

He learned how to milk the cows, but when it came to be killing a chicken for his mother to cook, he just couldn't do it. He loved animals and didn't want them to be killed for any reason.

Levi said, "Joseph Levi, if we don't kill a chicken occasionally we wouldn't have food on the table." The boy would not eat any of the meat that his mother prepared. He would eat the vegetables but not the meat. When they passed the meat around the table, he wouldn't even look at it. His Mamma and Dad begin to worry about him and hoped in time he would change his mind.

He never did change his mind about eating meat. He loved the animals so much; he just couldn't imagine eating one. His Mamma was beside herself trying to get him to eat meat.

She started thinking: "Maybe I should buy some vitamins for him. Levi wouldn't approve because it is not our way. But I am worried about his health." Joseph Levi told her, "Mamma, you know how much I love animals. And you know I want to be a veterinarian when I grow up.

Please don't worry about me, I'll be ok." Sara Jane had tears in her eyes as he spoke. She wanted his dream of becoming a veterinarian to come true for her son, but with simply the prospect of an eighth grade education, she was doubtful. She worried he thought too much about being a veterinarian and tried to encourage him to help his father with his blacksmith trade. She was afraid he was going to be disappointed when he got out of school and couldn't do the things he had always dreamed about. Even at seven years old, he thought about the future all the time.

Chapter Twenty-Nine

After her car accident, Betty Anne was unable to go back to work in the flower shop right away. She felt tired most of the time, and the doctor said that her heart had gotten a little weaker than it was the last time he saw her. He added another prescription to her regimen and asked her to get as much rest as she could.

On a beautiful April afternoon in 1986, she was relaxing on the front porch of her home when she saw the mail-man coming down the street. She walked out to the mailbox to meet him.

They greeted each other, and he was on his way. She went through the mail and found a letter from New York City. Who in the world was Shelly Daniels in New York City? She returned to the porch where she could sit down and read the letter.

"Dear Mrs. Miller, I am a good friend of your daughter, Sadie Miller. She has longed to get in touch with you for a long time but was afraid you would not want anything to do with her. She is getting married in June to a fine man who is a pediatrician. She has put me in charge of sending out the wedding invitations, so I decided to invite you to the wedding. I know in my heart that she will be happy to see you, and I am hoping you will be able to come. Please come, Mrs. Miller, Sadie needs her Mother to be there. The ceremony is Saturday, June 7, 1986 at 2:00 in the afternoon. It will be held at the First
Baptist Church of New York."
265 W 79th Street
New York, NY 10024
Sincerely Shelly Daniels

Betty Anne couldn't believe what she just read. She read the letter over and over as tears rolled down her face. The two women she had ever spoken to about her Sadie and Danny, were her friend Barbara and Sara Jane. She wondered what they would think and decided to call

Barbara, who came over to see Betty Anne as soon as she hung up the phone. Betty Anne showed Barbara the letter and watched her face as she read it. Barbara didn't know what to say at first and then looked at her. Barbara said. "Betty Anne, you have got to go to the ceremony."

Betty Anne knew how weak her heart was, and she didn't know if she could make the trip. She lay awake that night thinking about the letter and thought this was the first sign that Sadie was alive and well in over eight years; and now she was getting married.

The next morning, she made an appointment with her heart doctor to discuss her making a trip down to New York. He said. "You will ultimately have to have surgery on your heart to repair some heart valves; you can't keep putting it off. If you take the trip someone goes with you. Just in case something should happen. You could get sick and need a doctor. I am against the trip you are taking, and I will not be responsible if something should happen to you, such as a heart attack."

Something inside of her kept telling her to take the trip. She wanted to see her daughter, and this was an opportunity she couldn't pass up. She decided to ask Barbara to go with her. She told her she would pay all her expenses if she would go. Barbara said, "Betty Anne, that's not necessary because I was going to go with you anyway. Somebody's got to keep an eye on you."

It was a lovely day for a ride in the country, so Betty Anne decided to go see Sara Jane and see what she thought of the letter. April landscapes were blooming with flowers, and the fields were green with the fresh new grass of the year. As she got closer to the Amish

Community she could see the horse and buggies trotting up and down the dirt roads. As she passed them she waved and continued to go calmly down the road. She thought about the time

Sara Jane and Levi's buggy got run off the road, and she didn't want to cause anyone to get hurt.

As she approached their farm, she saw Levi out in the field with his horse plowing the land. He was planting the seeds for the corn and beans he had planned on growing. The boys were out playing in the front yard, and Sara Jane was sitting on the front porch peeling apples.

When they saw Betty Anne's car coming down the road, they all got excited and ran to meet her as she drove onto the property. They hugged her and said how happy they were to see her.

The children return to their playing as the two women walked into the kitchen.

She gave her a cup of hot tea and a piece of apple pie that she had just made that morning.

The house always smelled so good from her friends baking and had a warmth about it that seemed calming. She spoke low to her as if someone was listening. She took the letter out of her coat pocket and handed it to her. Sara Jane opened the envelope and began to read the letter. She looked up at her and said, "How exciting, you definitely know where your daughter is. You are going to go aren't you, dear? You can't miss out on the opportunity to see her!" Betty Anne looked grave and said, "I have been having some medical problems, and the doctor advised me not to take the trip. But I'm stubborn, you know, and I must go, or I may never get another chance to see my daughter."

Chapter Thirty

Sara Jane didn't want to pry into Betty Anne's business, but she wanted to know what kind of medical problems she had been having. Her friend continued, "I have decided to go to New York, and my neighbor Barbara is going with me." Sara Jane said, "I feel a lot better and I'm happy Barbara is going with you. But I'm still concerned about the medical problems you have." She decided Betty Anne would tell her when she was ready to. They hugged and said their goodbyes, and she drove home to Ruby Hope. She was left with unanswered questions about Betty Anne's medical condition again.

As the days passed, Betty Anne was counting them down; she was so happy that she was going to see her daughter after almost eight years. Her heart was weak, and she felt so tired all the time, but she was determined to take the trip to New York. She didn't want to fly, so, she decided they would take the train. They drove to the nearest station where they boarded the train. This would take them into New York, and from there they would get a taxi. She was so nervous that she could hardly breathe and wasn't sure that she should even be there. She looked out of the train window and tried to imagine what Sadie's life was like.

Sadie didn't know her mother had been invited to the wedding, but in her heart, she wished her mother could be there with her on her special day. She had been missing her mother for a long time but didn't have the nerve to call her. At the same time, she had been thinking her mother was mad at her for leaving Ruby Hope Valley. Betty Anne and Barbara sat in the back of the church during the ceremony. She never even saw them. During the reception,

Sadie's friend Shelly came up to her and said, "hey, have you seen your mother yet?" She looked shocked and started looking around for her. Shelly kept talking. "I sent her an invitation, Sadie, because I knew you wouldn't." She was very surprised to hear this.

Betty Anne and Barbara were standing by the door when Betty Anne heard a voice say "Mother." She looked around and saw her daughter coming toward her with tears in her eyes. She started to cry too as they hugged each other. Sadie whispered, "Mother, I love you, and I am so sorry; please forgive me."

She introduced Betty Anne and Barbara to her new husband, James Roland. He had a kind face and was very handsome. Betty Anne knew that Sadie had made a good choice.

After the reception, Sadie said, "When I get back from my honeymoon, I am going to come to see you in Ruby Hope. She promised she would never be out of touch with her again. Betty Anne felt that this was the happiest day of her life; she assuredly got her daughter back.

Before they left to go to the train station, someone tapped her on the shoulder. As she turned around, she saw her son Danny standing there with a young woman beside him. She could hardly believe her eyes as they looked at each other. She hugged him and said, "Oh, Danny, it's so good to see you. You look handsome and all grown up." He then introduced her to his wife,

Judy. He said, "Mother, how have you been?" "Missing my son and daughter," she replied. He looked at her calmly, and he said, "I have been traveling all over the world with my job. I'm sorry I haven't gotten in touch with you for so long." Long, she thought to herself -- that's an understatement -- and she reminded him it had been almost eight years since she saw him last.

She couldn't believe how cold he seemed toward her and thought she was going to cry.

She held it back as if she could. She thought to herself, "I know in my heart I haven't done anything to make him so cool toward me. He was the one that left home and never contacted me. He was the one that broke my heart and made me cry a million times." She was happy to see him and meet his wife but wondered if she would ever see him again.

She didn't know these people and wondered what had happened to them since they left home. There was so much she wanted to know about them, but she knew she might never know.

As they rode back on the train, she couldn't help but think, "I wonder why I was even invited to the ceremony. Sadie seemed happy to see me, but even she seemed distant, and Danny was someone I didn't even know." She thought about Sara Jane and her family. "I love them so much. They have always been there for me. At least I have them and my good friend and neighbor, Barbara in my life. I am truly blessed to have friends like these because God knew I needed them."

After Betty Anne and Barbara arrived back in Ruby Hope, she was exhausted and had to lie down. Her heart was beating so fast, and she felt anxious. Thinking back on the wedding and seeing her son and daughter had almost made her ill. They didn't know about her heart condition, nor did they even ask about her health.

Subsequently Betty Anne's heart condition grew worse, and the doctor became stern with her: "You need surgery to correct the problem. You can't keep putting it off; it must be now or never." Betty Anne had not said anything to Sara Jane because she knew she would worry. So, she told Barbara that she had let the doctor schedule surgery.

Chapter Thirty-One

One day soon after, whilst Sara Jane was in town at the market, she ran into Barbara.

She said, "How is Betty Anne doing since the trip? I haven't heard from her since she attended the wedding." Barbara was a hesitant at first and didn't know if she should tell her about the surgery or not. She knew how close the two of them were and decided she should know what was going on. So, she said, "She saw her son and daughter and was disappointed in them. It was too much for her, and she shouldn't have gone. She has been sick for some time now with a bad heart." If she had just known something bad was wrong with her friend, but she was praying

Betty Anne would sooner or later tell her. She understood her friend's need to be reserved, but she was beside herself. She asked Barbara not to let her know she had told her. Barbara agreed to keep their meeting to herself.

In August She checked into the hospital to have her open-heart surgery. She was having some valves repaired that had not been working as they should. When she woke up from the surgery, Sara Jane was sitting by her bed holding her hand. She was surprised to see her, but pleased she was there. It took about a year for Betty Anne to get her strength back completely. During that time, Sara Jane and Barbara were always around helping to take care of her. She felt so blessed to have friends like these two women and wished there was some way she could repay them for their kindness. She said a silent prayer that maybe, just maybe, she would hear from her daughter soon.

Fall passed, and then the winter came to the Valley. The weather was once again very cold and snowy. She couldn't come out to see Betty Anne because of the snow and ice on the ground. The roads were treacherous with falling limbs and debris. She said to Levi, "I believe it has snowed every year if I remember right. The fields look covered in the snow, and it makes it hard for our community to get out and go anywhere." The horses couldn't travel safely on ice and snow, and it was dangerous for the buggies to be on the road during these times.

By spring's first days Betty Anne was ready to go outside; she wanted to start going to the quilting groups again. She missed her Amish friends and her extended family. She was feeling so much better since her surgery last summer and felt like she could at last be herself again. Sara Jane called Betty Anne from the phone booth and asked her if she felt like coming out to the quilting gathering. She said, "Maggie - - Caleb's wife -- is having them at her house now and all the Amish ladies would love to see you." She was glad to hear from her and said, "I'm feeling just fine and ready to get out of the house. I was just thinking about coming out to the quilting gathering."

As she drove to Maggie's farm, she sat back and enjoyed all the beautiful green fields she passed. The men were hard at work baling hay and planting their seeds. Even the young boys were working alongside their fathers. She started thinking about Sadie and

Danny again and seemed to remember her daughter saying she was going to come see her. It had been almost a year since she attended the ceremony and still no word from either one of them.

Danny was so distant that day, she felt it was hopeless to think he would ever come to see her again. He had his traveling job and a new wife, and that was all that mattered to him. She was hurt deeply but knew in her heart she would never give up on him.

When she arrived at Maggie's, Betty Anne was greeted by several of the Amish women.

They were excited to see her again and hoped she was feeling well. Maggie said, "We are going to start on another wedding quilt – this one is for Mattie Sue and Samuel." Betty Anne said, "I am so happy to hear about Samuel. He is a very nice young man, and Mattie Sue is a lucky girl. I am excited to help you ladies with the quilt. When do we get started?" Sara Jane had brought the two boys. The older kids took the boys outside to play games while the ladies quilted.

Maggie's house smelled so good, as usual she had been baking a cake. The scents of apple and cinnamon filled the air and made Betty Anne hungry. Maggie had apple pie ready for the ladies along with a big scoop of vanilla ice cream made from the milk of their very own cows.

The quilt was large, but the ladies managed it with no problem. It had beautiful dark colors in it, according to their custom. The reds, dark greens, and dark blues intertwined with each other and made a beautiful design. Betty Anne said, "Mattie Sue is going to love this quilt.

The colors are lovely and should brighten up any room. "After she said that, she felt a bit self-conscious; she knew these women didn't have bright colors in their homes. But no one seemed to take offense.

Chapter Thirty-Two

Sara Jane and Levi were excited that his brother was getting married and planned to have the wedding at the farm. Samuel had grown into a fine young man, as good a blacksmith now as Levi. His brother was a good teacher to him, and they both had a solid business going together. Mattie Sue came from a large Amish family with three sisters. She was the youngest of the girls and the last one to get married in her family. Samuel had found a nice house on a couple of acres. The barn was small like the one Levi had when he first got married. But since he worked at Levi's farm, he didn't need a big barn.

The wedding was going to be in June 1987. She was anxious to get started with the plans. Sara Jane truly liked Mattie Sue and knew they would be good friends. Levi and

Samuel worked all day in their shop, but took time each day to help get the house ready for the ceremony. She was busy baking and taking care of the two boys, but she would take time to help them. They took everything out of the big living room and replaced it with benches.

They had already cleaned the walls and floors and taken care of the yards. Samuel was a hard working young man, and Levi was proud of him. Instead of having the women from the community come and do the cleaning, the two men did it all themselves.

Sara Jane cooked them a hot meal every night. They were always exhausted and sweaty, so, she would have them wash up good before they could sit down at the table. Levi and Samuel headed straight to bed after dinner because they got up at five am every morning.

She was surprised how well they cleaned up the yards and the front room. All she had to do now was bake the wedding cake. She loved baking cakes and started thinking about the time she went with Betty Anne to the big Flea Market to sell her cakes. She decided when all this was over she was going to do that again.

Mattie Sue decided to wear her blue Amish dress with her white apron and kappa.

All the bridesmaids and grooms would wear blue, too. She had asked her three sisters to be in their wedding, and of course Levi would be Samuel's best man. Her flower garden was bursting with flowers of all colors. The yards had been cut, and the front porch was decorated with beautiful white ribbons made by the ladies from the quilting group.

She had invited Betty Anne and knew this time she didn't have to ask permission for her to come. All the community loved and respected her dear friend and always looked forth to seeing her at their quilting group. Betty Anne decided to give the couple a beautiful blue tablecloth that was crocheted around the bottom. She knew that Mattie Sue's favorite color was blue, and she would love it. It had been special made for her at one of the finer stores in Ruby Hope Valley.

The couple had been seeing each other for a year now. They were going to be baptized into the Amish church the day before the ceremony. Everyone in the community came out to see them get baptized. All you could hear was talk of the ceremony. Sara Jane was busy trying to bake as many things as she could. She had already made a beautiful cake and decided to bake a few pies. The house looked beautiful, and the aroma coming from the kitchen was delightful. Samuel could hardly believe how lucky he was to have his sister in law and brother taking care of all the details. Mattie Sue had enough to take care of and was truly grateful to Levi and Sara Jane for letting them have the matrimony at their home.

The wedding day came, and everyone in the party dressed in blue. The girls had blue dresses, white aprons, and each wore a white kappa. The men wore blue shirts and black suits.

The front of the house was full of her Amish friends and Betty Anne. She Said, "I will sit with the boys and keep them as quiet as I can." The boys had on little black suits with black straw hats. They looked adorable to her, and she couldn't help but smile to herself.

Chapter Thirty-Three

The wedding lasted for almost thirty minutes. Everyone then lined up at the long table

Levi had set up on the front porch. The women had prepared a delicious lunch for everyone: fried chicken, mac and cheese, potato salad, pickles, beets, biscuits, and all sorts of deserts. After everyone had eaten, she brought out the cake. Betty Anne said, "That is the most beautiful cake I have ever seen. "I believe you outdid yourself this time." She had picked roses from her garden and placed them all around the bottom of the cake. It was just too pretty to eat, thought Betty

Anne. After everyone had gone home, she was exhausted, so she stayed for a time and helped get the boys ready for bed.

As she drove home from the farm, she thought about the wedding. Samuel and Mattie

Sue's reminded her of when Levi and Sara Jane got married almost ten years earlier. It was a beautiful wedding, very different from the traditional ones she had gone to before?

She thought they made a lovely couple and wished for them to have happiness and a blessed life together.

As always, Sadie and Danny came to mind, and she started wishing she would hear from them. When she got home, she was very tired and decided to go to bed early. She was going to start back to work in the flower shop the next day, and she needed her rest. She decided she would tell her boss she could only work two or three days a week. Six days a week was too much for a sixty-three-year-old woman. Besides, she had decided she wanted more time to spend volunteering with the youngsters at the orphanage.

When she got home, she found she had received a telegram from her daughter; she was surprised, and tears began to roll down her face. Betty Anne seemed to shed tears at almost anything these days; she just couldn't hold them back. It had been almost two years since she had gone to the wedding. She had thought she would never see or hear from her daughter again.

The telegram said that she was coming home "with a surprise" for her mother. She called

Barbara over to tell her the good news. Betty Anne didn't understand what it meant by surprise.

It said she would be here on Friday.

Betty Anne was terribly excited and said, "Barbara, I have so much to do to get ready for her visit. The house needs to be cleaned, the guest room bed needs fresh sheets, and

I need to cook something she loves." She remembered that as a little girl, Sadie had loved mac and cheese and fried pork chops. "I'll go to the grocery store and buy the things I need to make her a good meal." Barbara was concerned about her friend overdoing it, and said, "Betty Anne,

I will help you clean the house and do whatever you need done. You need to calm yourself and relax before you have a breakdown. Remember your health is important."

The next morning, Barbara showed up at seven to get started on cleaning the house. She said, "Well, here I am ready to work." She swept and mopped the kitchen, changed the linen on the bed in the guest bedroom and cleaned the bathroom. Betty Ann couldn't believe what Barbara had done for her. She said. "Barbara, you are an amazing friend.

Come on, let's go to town; I want to buy you a nice lunch before I report to work."

"A friend loves at all times" Proverbs 17:17

Betty Anne was so excited that she almost forgot to tell Sara Jane about Sadie's visit. When she drove out to the farm the next evening, the boys were very happy to see her again. They hugged and sat down on the front porch as she told her friend that her daughter was coming home on Friday. She was almost out of breath when she spoke.

Sara Jane marveled at the wonderful surprise and said, "I am so pleased for you. Levi and I will say a special prayer that everything will work out ok for you." The days that followed were happy for Betty Anne; she could hardly believe her daughter was coming home.

Chapter Thirty-Four

At five o'clock on Friday afternoon a black car pulled up in front of the house.

Barbara was sitting in the living room with Betty Anne trying to keep her calm. Sadie stepped out of the car with a baby in her arms. Betty Anne saw them coming and ran to the door to open it. She stood there with the baby as she smiled at her Mother. Betty Anne had tears rolling down her face as she looked at her daughter and then the baby. As they walked into the house, she introduced her to Barbara. Sadie said. "Mother meet your new Granddaughter. Her name is

Emily Grace." Betty Anne took the baby in her arms and cradled her to her chest. She still had tears rolling down her face as Barbara and Sadie watched her.

Once they settled the baby in her comfortable travel bed, Betty Anne hugged her daughter as if she would never let her go again. They sat up almost all night just talking about what had taken place through the years since Sadie left home, all the while laughing, crying, and looking at old pictures. They ate cookies, candy, and drink soft drinks until they thought they were going to burst. Betty Anne thought this was the happiest time of her life and wished it would never end. Sadie said. "My husband has gone on a business trip for the hospital. so, I thought this would be the perfect time to visit. I wanted to bring Emily Grace to meet her Grandmother."

Emily Grace was six months old and the most adorable baby she had ever seen. Betty Anne couldn't hold her enough; Sadie said, "Mother, you are spoiling her." "I know, but isn't that what grandmothers are supposed to do? Sadie, I have become friendly with an Amish family. Would you like to ride out to their farm and meet them? My friends, Sara Jane and Levi, have two young sons, Joseph

Levi and Samuel John. When Joseph Levi was four, the doctors discovered he had kidney failure. His father gave him one of his kidneys. Both are doing well. I can't wait for you to meet them." She spoke of them at length, and Sadie was very interested in meeting the Amish family, she had heard so much about.

The following day, they rode out to the farm for a visit. Sara Jane and the boys greeted Betty Anne with their usual enthusiasm, and the kids came running up to meet her.

Sadie was truly surprised and glad her mother had such nice friends. Betty Anne couldn't wait for Sara Jane to see Emily Grace. She took her from Sadie and handed the baby to her friend. Sara Jane said, "This is the cutest baby I have ever seen. I would love to have a girl.

Please come into the kitchen and have a cup of tea." She had been baking again, and the house was suffused with the scent of apples and cinnamon.

The three women sat in the kitchen just talking and laughing about things that had happened since Sara Jane and Betty Anne met. Sara Jane said, "Betty Anne has been like a mother to me, and I love her very much." Sadie didn't know what to think, but suddenly a guilty feeling came over her. She knew in her heart that she had done wrong by not staying in contact with her Mother all these years. Tears began to well up in her eyes.

They had visited for about an hour when Betty Anne said, "We need to get back to Ruby Hope. It's almost time to feed the baby. And I want to spend as much time as I can with them during the time they are visiting." Sara Jane understood but was a little disappointed that they had to leave. She gave them a whole apple pie to take with them. She had just baked it that morning. As they drove back to Ruby Hope, Sadie said. "Mother, I' sorry I wasn't a better daughter to you. But I am happy you have Sara Jane and her family in your life.

They seem like a wonderful family." "They are the best friends anyone could have."

The day came for Sadie and Emily Grace to leave; Betty Anne was heartbroken they had to go. Sadie said, "Mother, I will never be out of touch with you again. I want you to know that I've always loved you."

They hugged and hugged, and the tears began to roll down their cheeks.

Betty Anne whispered in Sadie's ear, "I've never stopped loving you and praying you would come back to me." Then they were gone again, but Betty Anne had hope in her heart now and looked in advance to hearing from her often.

Chapter Thirty-Five

About two weeks later, she got a letter from Sadie along with a picture of Emily Grace. She was delighted to receive the letter and promptly wrote back. From then on, they stayed in touch with each other, and Sadie continued to send pictures of Emily Grace. Betty Anne had never mentioned Danny to Sadie, so she decided to ask her about him. Sadie just said he was a busy man, traveling all over the place, and that she hardly ever heard from him.

She sent her mother his address and asked her to write to him. Betty Anne was hesitant at first but decided she would write to him; after all he was her son.

She wrote a letter to Danny. It said:

"I wish I could hear from you, Danny. Sadie and
Emily Grace came to see me. We had a wonderful visit. I was so happy to
see them. I would love to see you and put my arms around you. I will always
love you, son. I miss you more each day.
Love, Mother"

She had not mentioned her heart condition to Sadie, and she wasn't about to tell Danny.

She said to herself, "I pray he will respond to my letter. If he doesn't, I won't worry about it anymore; it's time to move on with my life." A month passed after she sent the letter to Danny, and still no word came from him. She was content in the fact that Sadie and Emily Grace were back in her life now.

She knew Danny was an Architect and traveled all over the world for his employer. He was rarely at home, and it had caused him and his wife to get a divorce; thankfully, they never had children. About another month rolled by, when she received a telegram from Danny's ex-wife:

"I'm sorry to have to tell you this, but Danny was killed in an automobile accident in Australia. I'll let you know details regarding his body as soon as the Australian authorities release it into my custody, and it can be shipped home."

Betty Anne couldn't believe what she just read. The message had no feelings whatsoever, and it was short and to the point. She said, "Who is this woman? Does she not care this is Danny? Betty Anne was devastated and felt like she was going to faint. She said, "Danny dead, this can't be true, not my Danny." The words sounded alien. She murmured them over and over.

She finally got the strength to call Barbara to come over. She knew she needed someone with her. Barbara came over and stayed with her all night. She tried to console her, but Betty Anne couldn't stop crying.

Barbara reminded her of Sadie, Emily Grace, and Sara Jane. She said, "Betty Anne, you have so many persons that love you, and you must think of them now. You can't give up, you have too much to live for. It will take a long time, but it will get better. You need to surround yourself with these folks that love you." Barbara refused to leave her until she was able to stay by herself. She knew she had to get in touch with Sara Jane. The following day Sadie called Barbara. She said, "I'm coming to home to help Mother with the funeral arrangements. The company Danny worked with is shipping his body home to Ruby Hope. Would you please keep a close eye on her for me until I can get there?" "Yes, Sadie I will be glad to. I'm going to stay with her tonight. She doesn't need to be alone." "Thank you, Barbara, I don't know what Mother would do without you. You are a good friend and neighbor."

Sadie arrived a few days later and helped Betty Anne with all the funeral arrangements for her brother. They had a beautiful service for him and even some of the Amish community came to the funeral. Sara Jane, Levi, Samuel, and Mattie Sue came and sat with Betty Anne and Sadie. Betty Anne was pleased to see her Amish friends. She needed the comfort of knowing they were there for her. Sadie stayed for a week with her mother before she had to go back to New York. Her husband and his mother were taking care of the baby, and she needed to go see about her. Betty Anne hated to see Sadie leave but knew she needed to go home to her family. They hugged and whispered their love for each other. She felt so much better just knowing she had Sadie back in her life now.

Chapter Thirty-Six

Several weeks later, Betty Anne decided she would go back to work again. She had not worked since before the funeral. She thought it might help her to cope with her life. She was having a hard time just getting out of the bed every day. It was a struggle for her to do just about anything; she needed something to keep her busy.

Sara Jane and Levi decided to have a small get together for Betty Anne to show her how much everyone in the Amish community cared for her. Summer was coming to an end, and they wanted to have a picnic outside in the yard, so Levi and Samuel set up several tables and benches in the side yard where the flower garden was. The Amish women had been baking for days for the occasion. They baked cakes, pies, and several casseroles, such as mac and cheese; they prepared potato salad, fried chicken, and baked beans.

Betty Anne was delighted to be able to go out to the farm and asked her if she could bring Barbara with her. She was more than happy for her to come, and she knew the community would not mind.

Late one August afternoon, Betty Anne and Barbara rode out to the farm for the picnic.

They thought there would simply be a few Amish folks there, but were surprised to see the whole Amish community. They were standing around the table waiting for her with a smile on their faces. She was so happy to see everyone and thanked them for coming out for her.

They all knew she had been going through a hard time and just wanted to lift her spirits. She had such a good time that day and began to feel like a human being once more. She had her church friends in town, but she also had all these wonderful Amish families.

She went back to work at the flower shop the following week, but there wasn't a day that she didn't think of Danny. He had been gone for nine years now and ultimately came home in a casket. He was buried in the cemetery behind the Ruby Hope Valley Church. Betty Anne visited frequently. As she stood over his grave, she started thinking about Danny when he was a little boy. All the while tears were falling down her face. She remembered that he had gone to this church every Sunday as a boy and was an active member of his Sunday school class. He used to rehearse his Bible verses with her. She smiled as she thought, "He was a good boy and was always telling me he loved me. He would say, 'Mama, I love you a bushel and a peck.' I would say to him, same here my munchkin, then we would both laugh until we almost cried."

I would be in the kitchen cooking, she remembered, and Danny would come in and stand on my feet holding on to me around my waist. I would have to walk around the kitchen with him hanging on to me. I will never understand what happened to him. Why did he leave Ruby Hope and never come back? How can you love someone and turn your back on them?

As days and weeks rolled by, she began to feel better and wanted to try and get her life back. She had not been out to see the Click family since the picnic, which had been in August. It was now November and starting to get very cold. She thought she would go out to see them before the snow came, as it always did in the Valley.

As she drove out to the farm, she thought of all the things that had happened this past year.

Sadie and the baby came to see her, and she lost her son for always: one happy situation and one very sad situation. She thought, "*There is nothing worse than losing a child*. I will always stay in touch with Sadie and never let her out of my life again." As always, Sara Jane welcomed Betty Anne and invited her into the kitchen where they could sit and talk. Of course she had been baking as she did every day. She offered Betty Anne a cup of hot tea and a blueberry muffin she had baked. They spoke about the quilting group coming up next spring.

Sara Jane said, "Betty Anne, I hope we can go to the big market and sell cakes."

She knew she needed to get Betty Anne's mind off her son and back to doing the things she loved.

"I would love to do all those things, and I hope I will be able to do them," Betty Anne replied. She had a sad expression on her face as she said, "I haven't been feeling very well since Danny died. I was hoping I would be better by spring." The grief and despair she felt in her life was overwhelming, making her feel useless. It was making her physically and mentally ill.

She could see that no matter what she suggested, her friend wasn't going to give it an effort. All she could do was pray for her and hope that she would get better.

Snow came to Ruby Hope as it always did in December. The roads and streets were covered. Limbs and debris were strewn all over the ground. Betty Anne didn't have much desire to go out and Christmas shop this year. The town was lit up with beautiful Christmas lights and decorations. The big Christmas tree sat right in the middle of town as always. She wanted to get Sadie and the baby a Christmas gift, but she found she didn't have the strength to get dressed. The spirit of Christmas was gone, and all she wanted to do was stay in the house.

Chapter Thirty-Seven

The snow had let up, and the sun was shining brightly one afternoon. Barbara came over to see if she could talk her into going shopping together. Betty Anne didn't want to go, but she was persistent, so she decided to go along. They had a very good time that day walking around window shopping and stopping at the local coffee shop. She bought a few gifts and said, "Barbara, I will try to get in the Christmas spirit." Barbara said, "I will come over and help you put up your Christmas tree and few decorations. It will help you get in the spirit of Christmas." Betty Anne wasn't very pleased about it, but she said it would be ok.

Sara Anne had invited her to spend Christmas day with them at the farm. Betty Anne wanted to go, but she was so depressed, she didn't think she could. On Christmas morning she changed her mind and decided she would go. She got dressed and made her way to her car. The ground was slippery, and she almost fell. She thought to herself, "I sure hope the roads are not going to be this icy."

She did miss seeing the boys and all the family. She felt she needed to be around this loving family. Everyone was there, including the newlyweds, Samuel and Mattie Sue. Mark said a silent prayer as he always did before a meal. Betty Anne said her own silent prayer: "God, please help me to get over this depression I'm in so I can begin to feel like myself once more."

After Christmas was over, Betty Anne began to feel much better. Being around friends at work every day was a big help to her. At last spring arrived, and the flowers started to shoot up out of the ground. Beautiful tulips, irises, and at last roses began to bloom all around the town and farm lands. By April 1988 it seemed like time had flown by since the funeral. She continued to get letters and pictures from Sadie.

One letter said, "The baby is beginning to walk and talk and jabbers all the time." Betty Anne was always happy to hear from Sadie and wished she could see her and the baby.

Betty Anne and Sara Jane decided to bake cakes and take them to the flea market as they had when they first became friends. They baked and frosted six cakes. Betty Anne said that would be enough. They loaded them up in her car and headed out to the market. They had a very good day and sold all the cakes. Betty Anne thought it was a fun day and wished they could come more often. The market had all kinds of Amish furniture and tools the Amish men had made. You could find anything you wanted there. She decided the next time Sadie came, she would bring her out to the market and get her a beautiful Amish quilt.

On her ride home, she enjoyed looking at the farm land. It was always so beautiful, and you could see all the Amish kids out playing or helping their fathers in the fields.

Samuel and Mattie Sue had announced at Christmas that they were having a baby. Betty Anne thought, "I want to give them something special for the baby, but I need to talk to Sara Jane first.

She would know what to give them."

Sara Jane told Betty Anne that she had a miscarriage. She said, "I want to try again as soon as I can. I want a girl so bad." Betty Anne was worried about her and said, "Sara Jane, you should wait a while before trying again." Over the next year, though, she had three miscarriages. Betty Anne spoke with Levi and suggested she go to a doctor in the city and be examined. He was against it at first, but he knew how wise Betty Anne was and agreed for her to take her to a doctor. After all, he thought, if it had not been for Betty Anne suggesting we take Joseph Levi to a doctor in town, he might not be alive today.

Betty Anne took Sara Jane to see her gynecologist the following week. The gynecologist, Lucy Bradshaw, did a full work up on her. She told her that she was going to need to have a hysterectomy. She didn't understand what that meant, so they called Betty Anne into the office to explain it to her. After she explained the situation to her, she said, "You need to do what the doctor has advised you to do. You won't be able to have any more babies after the surgery, but your health cannot stand all these miscarriages." Sara Jane's eyes swelled up with tears when she heard this. She had been longing to have one more child, and now she couldn't.

As they drove home, Betty Anne tried to console her, saying, "You will feel much better after the surgery. I am so sorry, Sara Jane, but God knows what's best for us. At least you have Joseph Levi and Samuel John." After dropping Sara Jane off at the farm, she walked out to the barn and talked with Levi about the surgery. Levi thanked Betty Anne for taking her to the doctor. He said, "I don't know what we would do without you."

A Poem by Esther Keim / October 4, 2017
My Children
In the night I hear a cry.
When I wake up I think I'd rather die,
and then I think of those that aren't as fortunate as I.
To wake up in the middle of the night to hear my baby cry.

Chapter Thirty-Eight

On the drive home, Betty Anne thought about all that had happened, and she knew in her heart she was needed. She had a purpose now. Levi and Sara Jane were her family, along with her daughter, Sadie and baby Emily Grace. She thought how lucky she was to have all these folks in her life. The grief she felt was a like a veil that hung around her heart every minute of the day, but she decided right then that she was going to try to help citizens who needed to get through rough times in their lives, such as Sara Jane. Her friend was going to need her support to get through the surgery. Betty Anne knew she would be depressed afterwards. She wanted another child, and now she couldn't have one.

On a lovely afternoon in August 1988, Mattie Sue gave birth to a fine baby boy; they named him Ethan Nathaniel Click. The baby weigh seven pounds when he was born and had a head full of blond hair. Samuel was very proud of Ethan Nathaniel and couldn't stop talking about him. Levi said, "I'm so happy for you Samuel. I'm proud of my two sons, Joseph Levi and Samuel John, and I thank God for them every day. I'm broken hearted for Sara Jane, though. But I know the Lord knows what's best."

Sara Jane had the hysterectomy and recovered very well, although she was depressed for several months afterwards. Betty Anne was always by her friend's side during these difficult days. She comforted her and prayed with her. She always reminded her of her two precious boys. She also reminded her of what Joseph Levi had gone through and how lucky they were that he received his father's kidney. She was fortunate to have Betty Anne in her life, and she subsequently began to come out of her depression. She hugged her two sons and told them how much she loved them, and from then on, she began to be herself.

She started baking and canning. She decided, "if it's God's will that I don't have any more babies, then that's the way it's going to be." She enjoyed Samuel and Mattie Sue's happiness and doted on little Ethan Nathaniel. It seemed to fill an emptiness she felt inside. They just lived two miles down the road from them, so, she took the boys down to see them as often as she could.

Fall had come to the Valley, and the fields were still green, but the leaves on the trees had started to turn colors. They were so pretty with their mixture of gold, brown, green, and yellow leaves. A few leaves had started to fall from the trees, and there was a slight coolness in the air. She was feeling much better and loved this time of year. She would get out in the yard and rake a big pile of leaves up so the boys could run and jump right in the middle of them. She decided she would walk down to the public phone booth located out in the field and give Betty Anne a call. She wanted to see how she was doing and invite her to come to dinner one evening before the cold set in. Betty Anne was surprised and glad to hear from her. She said. "I would love to come out and have dinner one evening." She decided she would invite her Dad, John, and her grandparents. She thought the following Sunday evening would be a good time.

The following week Grandpa Abram passed away at eighty-nine years of age; his heart just gave out. The family was heartbroken and decided to bury him on the farm. Mark wanted his father to be near Ruth, his mother. The Amish community all came out to attend the funeral. Many buggies lined the road leading to Mark's house. Three hundred people came to the funeral that day. Sara Jane said, "Grandpa would have been so proud to see all those buggies out front."

The women brought all kinds of food for the folks to eat after the service. Grandpa Abram was laid to rest in a plain pine box that Mark made himself. It wasn't typical of the Amish to bury them on their land, but Mark wanted his family close to him and just couldn't put grandpa in a public cemetery.

Grandmother Ruth was unable to attend the service because she was too frail and weak herself. She was eighty-seven years old and could hardly get around anymore. Sara Jane decided not to have the Sunday dinner; her heart just wasn't in it right now. She had just started to feel better and had Betty Anne to thank for that because she was suffering from depression herself. She still wanted to do something nice for her, but it would have to wait for now.

Chapter Thirty-Nine

After Grandpa Abram passed away Betty Anne decided to drive out to the farm to see how she was doing. On her drive to the country, she started reminiscing about when she first met Sara Jane, thinking aloud: "The Amish women had started piecing a quilt for her.

We sat next to each other and began a conversation that has led to a lifelong friendship. I thought she was one of the sweetest young women I had ever met. I learned how to quilt that day and how they pieced the different materials together. Over the years since, we have experienced so many ups and downs in our lives but have always been there for one another. I can't think of a better friend in the world."

As she drove down the dirt roads, she passed several farms, a few were big and a few were small. She could see the men still working around their barns and in the fields. Since it was getting cooler, the farmers were clearing the land, getting it ready for the winter months ahead.When she arrived at the farm, she saw Mark's buggy in front of the house and was worried that something had happened to Grandmother Ruth. Mark and John had just stopped by and she asked them to stay for dinner. They were happy to see Betty Anne and asked her to stay also. They had their dinner together after all, just slightly delayed.

Several times through the years Betty Anne had considered the prospect of joining the Amish church and becoming one of them. Even now it was still on her mind, and she thought she would talk to Sadie about it. The Amish folks had always been good to her, and she felt so peaceful whenever she was around them. Sara Jane and Levi thought of her as family and overlooked her worldly ways. They knew she was a Christian and a good person and had always been there for them whenever anything went wrong; that was all that mattered to them.

Joseph Levi and Samuel John were getting so big now that Betty Anne could hardly believe it. She had been preoccupied with other things of late, so much that she hadn't even noticed how they had grown. Joseph Levi was nine years old, and the picture of health. You would never know he was a sickly toddler. He was getting so tall and handsome and one of the sweetest boys she had ever known. He still didn't want to eat meat, and his mother and father couldn't understand it. While she was visiting the family, Joseph Levi came over to her and whispered in her ear. He said, "Betty Anne, I love animals and want to be a veterinarian when I grow up. All I really want to do is take care of the animals, and I just can't eat them." She was touched by his confiding in her. She told him, "I understand, and I will talk to your mother and father about it."

Levi expected his sons to follow in his footsteps when they got old enough. In fact, he wanted to teach Joseph Levi how to handle a hammer, and forge, but the child wasn't interested.

When he was just a boy, Levi had let him take care of the farm animals. He taught him a about blacksmithing too. So, he knew a lot about the trade already. Betty Anne knew this was going to be a problem for Levi. How would he ever understand that his son wanted to go away to school to become a veterinarian? Joseph Levi said, "Betty Anne I want to help my community with their animals." She said, "That is a wonderful thing to do, but it's a long way off, and you may change your mind – many times – before you are grown."

After dinner they all sat around discussing the weather and ordinary things going on in the Amish community. Sara Jane's brother John admitted he had met a lovely girl at one of the singings and wanted to start driving her around. Sara Jane told him he should go ahead and ask her out and see what happens. She asked him if she knew this girl and what her name was.

John was hesitant to say her name but belatedly told them. It was Rose Troyer, a relative of the Yoder family that lived down the road from Levi and Sara Jane. She was the cousin to Nan Yoder, who was married to one of the Yoder boys. Rose was visiting the Yoder family and had come from Lancaster County.

Sara Jane asked, "How long will she be visiting? Do you know if she has been baptized into the Amish Church?" John wished he had never even mentioned it at all. Now he had to answer all these questions, and he didn't feel very comfortable doing so. John continued to go to the singings on Sunday nights and met up with Rose. He knew she lived a long way away from Ruby Hope Valley, but he figured if they should get married she wouldn't mind moving to this beautiful town.

They drove around for several weeks when Rose told him, "I have to return to Lancaster County, John. Mother is concerned about me staying so long in Ruby Hope." John was disappointed and asked her when she would be returning. Rose said. "John, it may be several months before I can return here. He said, "I am sorry to hear that. I was hoping we might get engaged if you want to." She was surprised by this. "John, I'm real fond of you, but I'm not ready for marriage." "We could just stay engaged for a while," he said, "if that's what you want?" Rose knew her mother was not going to be happy about her running around with anyone who lived so far away. She knew that if they should decide to marry, she would have to move to Ruby Hope, and she didn't want that to happen. Mrs. Troyer was hoping when the time came for Rose to marry she would marry an Amish boy from the Lancaster community. John could see that this was going to be a problem so, he decided to talk with his sister about it.

Chapter Forty

That evening after everyone had gone, John stayed in the kitchen with her. He told her all about Rose. He said, "I genuinely love her, but I don't know what to do." Sara Jane looked worried and sat down at the kitchen table with a cup of tea in her hands. She said, "John, give Rose time and write to her often. If she cares for you she will be back; it may take a while, but she will come back." John felt better after talking with his sister, but he was still worried that he might never see Rose again.

The following week, following his sister's advice, John wrote a letter and said, "I will wait for you, Rose, and I pray you will come back to Ruby Hope soon."

Rose wrote back to John and said, "I will continue to write to you, but I don't know when I will be back for a visit with my cousin." John was disappointed in her letter to him. He wasn't sure what to think and decided he was going to Lancaster County.

John decided to talk with his father to tell him how he felt for Rose. He wanted to go to see her in Lancaster County. He was already twenty-three, and Rose was twenty, so he wanted to see whether she was ready for marriage. Mark said, "John, go ahead and take the trip, but be certain about Rose before you make any decisions of marriage. I will help you get a small farm of your own if you come back here to live. I don't want you to move to Lancaster County."

Mark knew how the heart works, and he reflected that if John were truly in love with Rose she might change his mind about a lot of things. John said, "I want to live here in Ruby Hope Valley, and I'm hoping she will come back with me."

John went to see his sister to tell her of his decision. He told her about his conversation with Dad and said that he truly wanted to live here with Rose if she would have him. A few days later, John called a taxi to come pick him up and take him to the train station. He began his journey to Lancaster County; he didn't know what to expect when he saw Rose. She didn't know John is coming and wasn't prepared for his visit. He had told her in his last letter that he might take a trip there but didn't say when.

Rose's mother wasn't pleased about the prospect of her daughter in a long distance relationship with this country boy. Upon arriving in Lancaster, John was very surprised to see a familiar face. Old Mr. Bieler, an Amish gentleman known to his family, had dropped off a visiting cousin at the train station, and he offered to take John out to their home. Rose was very taken aback to see John and seemed to have mixed feelings. She stepped outside the screen door onto the front porch, and said very soft, "Please just go wait for me out by the road. I don't want Mother to know you are here." She wanted Rose to marry anyone from their district, so she would stay in Lancaster County. John nodded, walked back to the road, and waited patiently.

It seemed like a very long time before Rose came out to the road. She said, "My Mother would not approve of me meeting you like this..." They spoke for a while, and John realized his impulsiveness coming to Lancaster had been foolish. There was no way Rose was going against her Mother's wishes. He said, "I'm going to take a taxi ride around the countryside, so I can get a good idea of what it looks like if for some reason I decide to stay here."

Rose tried to explain how she feels about her seeing anyone that doesn't live in Lancaster. They continued talking for a while and talked about them getting married. Rose still wasn't sure what to do even though they had been corresponding for months. Her mother was a strong willed Amish woman, who was very strict on her children. She didn't approve of marrying out of their district.

John said to Rose, "My Dad is going to help me get a small farm and a few animals. You would be happy in Ruby Hope Valley, Rose. The folks there are friendly and will always be there for you. You will love it, Rose, and you could go visit your family whenever you wanted to, I won't mind." She was impressed by his sincere honesty and felt a tear run down her face. In her heart she knew she truly cared for John, but she was afraid of her mother.

She didn't know how to tell her she wanted to marry him. John left to go home and still didn't have the answer he wanted. His heart felt heavy with sadness and longing for the woman he couldn't have.

Chapter Forty-One

After John came home from Lancaster County, he decided he would try to forget Rose.

Mark said soothingly, "Maybe in time, Rose will come around. John why don't we start looking for a small farm house?" John was eager to start looking. "I know everyone in this community, and if I put the word out, we will find what we're looking for." All John thought about was having his own little farm. He truly didn't care about it being small, if he had a garden and few animals.

It wasn't long before Mark heard from one of their close neighbors. A small farm had no more than a few days earlier come up for sale. It had a small house and a little red barn on it, just enough space for a couple to start with. Mark didn't need his youngest on the farm much anymore. Caleb and his family lived with Mark in the big house now. Caleb and Mathew helped with the duties, as Mark was getting on in age. John still helped his Dad on his place three to five days a week. Mark said to John. "I know you are excited about the place, and you will need time to work on it. Don't you worry about me; Caleb and Mathew will help this old man.

You concentrate on your new house." John responded with gratitude: "Thank you, Dad, but I want to still help you at least three days a week." "Ok, son do whatever you want. I know you are a hard worker, and I can always depend on you?"

Winter was ultimately coming to an end, and the days were growing warmer. Sara Jane and Levi decided to go and help John clean his farm house. She scrubbed the kitchen floors and washed down the walls. She put wood in the wood burning stove and started baking a pie and homemade bread. She wanted the house to be clean and comfortable for her little brother. John and Levi walked out to the barn and began cleaning it up. They put new boards up on the walls that had cracks in them and swept the floors clean. They climbed up on the roof and put new shingles on it. The roof had been patched before and had a few leaks. They were exhausted by the time they finished for the day.

Mark decided he would give John a few of his chickens, a cow, and a pig. John was excited to get the animals and couldn't thank his Dad enough. He was contented to have his own place now and kept hoping he would hear anything positive from Rose soon. He decided to write to her.

John wrote,

"Hi, Rose, I wanted to tell you about my new farm house. I've been doing a little work on it. Sara Jane and Levi came over and helped clean the house and repair the barn. It's a small house, Rose, but it's just right for me. Rose, I wish you would come for a visit. I miss you and can't wait for you to see my new place.

John

John reminded his Dad that he would come over to the farm three days a week and help him out. He needed to do a little bit for his Dad, for all he had done for him. Mark was glad for John to come over and help them. It was getting close to planting time, and they needed all the help that was available.

John decided to go to the big flea market and see if he might pick up a few things for the house. A few things he would build himself, but he needed a table and chairs for the kitchen and a few pots and pans. Sara Jane and Dad had given him a few items for the house, such as a bookcase, a few books, and a braided rug that his mother had made long before she died. He was thankful to his father and couldn't wait to get started on the little house. He genuinely wanted to impress Rose if she should come to visit her cousin this spring. John said, "Sara Jane, would you go with me to the flea market? I need to get a few things for the house. I need a few ideas from a woman -- you know, a woman's touch?" "Sure, John," she smiled. "I'd love to go. It reminds me of the time Betty Anne and I went to sell my cakes." She started thinking about her friend and wondered why she had not heard from her since Christmas.

She knew Betty Anne was still grieving over Danny even though she tried to hide it. She said to herself, "I think I will give her a call as soon as I can. I've been so busy trying to help John get settled in his new place. And the boys are growing up fast and need me more than ever." The boys were in school now. She didn't like them walking home unaccompanied, so she would take the buggy and go pick them up every day. She had her big brothers to walk with her when she was a child and always felt safe. There actually wasn't any one in the Amish community that she had to be afraid of, but she had always been a little over protective, maybe because of Joseph Levi's health or because she always had her brothers to protect her.

John and Sara Jane drove up to the big flea market and walked all around looking at all the furniture. They weren't supposed to have anything fancy, but John wanted to at least have a few pieces of furniture in his house that would attract Rose, such as a nice dresser for the bedroom and maybe a big sofa to sit on. He knew his sister was able to pick out the right furniture.

Chapter Forty-Two

Most of the furniture they looked at had been built by the Amish men in the community around them. She chose a dresser that was made of pine and had six drawers. It was perfect for the bedroom and would look great with his bed. She also selects a sofa and a matching chair that had cloth seating within a wooden frame that came up on each side, sleigh- like, almost like the ends of a bed. The cushioned seats were beige with dark brown and rust color swirled all through it; she thought it was a lovely piece of furniture. It didn't have fancy colors that stood out but was simple and pretty. John knew now why he wanted her to come with him; she had great taste, and he enjoyed her company.

Before leaving the flea market, they decided to stop by the candy shop. Sara Jane picked out chocolate fudge for her and Levi and few soft chews for the two boys. John had a hard time making up his mind but finally decided on the cotton candy. He told her he had not had any cotton candy since he was a little boy. They both laughed and started toward their buggy to go home. John decided with the proprietors to retrieve his furniture the following week. He said, "I'm going to need Levi and Caleb to help get the furniture home."

As they were walking toward their horse and buggy, they ran into Nan and Joseph Yoder.

John was surprised to see them, and asked Nan had she heard from Rose of late. Nan nodded and said, "She is coming for a visit. She will be here for a couple of weeks." "Oh, I didn't know she was coming. When will she be here?" Nan replied, "Next week anytime." Rose had stopped writing John, so he didn't know what to make of the news of her visit. They said their goodbyes and started toward the buggy. Sara Jane could see that John was upset about Rose. She said, "Do you need to talk about it?"

"No, I don't want to talk about it right now," he replied. On the way home, he was silent; all you could hear were the horse's hooves clip clopping as they went down the road.

As the days passed, John tried to put Rose out of his mind and work on his house. He decided to paint the outside while the weather was so nice. He heard in passing that Rose had arrived in town, but he wasn't going to go looking for her; she would have to come to him.

He was tired of chasing after her. One afternoon while he was outside painting his house, a buggy turned into his driveway. He saw that it was Nan and Rose. When it came to a stop, Rose stepped down from the buggy and walked over to John and said hello. She said, "I like your new house, John. I would love to see the inside." John tried to be nice to her and asked her to come in the house.

He was aware that the house looked attractive, with his new sofa and chair that he had bought at the flea Market. The bookcase from his father added to the pleasant quality of the house. It sat in the corner of the living room with several books in it. H showed her around the house and offered her a cup of tea. "No thanks, I don't want to keep Nan waiting too long," she replied. John said. "I know this place isn't very big, but I plan on having a better house one day, and this will do for now." Rose said, "I am very impressed with what you have done with this place. I'm happy for you, John. I hope to see you at the singings Saturday night." John decided not to comment on that and helped her up into the carriage.

As they guided the horses down the road, John just stood there looking at the back of the buggy until it disappeared. He was surprised at the way Rose acted; it was as if nothing had ever happened between them. The following day was Friday, and it was time for him to go to his family's home and help them. Planting season had begun, and his father was expecting him to help put in the seed. He worked so hard that he didn't have time to worry over his young woman.

Then Saturday came, and he was trying to make up his mind if he should go to the singing that night. He knew Rose would be there and might expect him to give her a ride in his buggy. There was no sense, he thought, in trying to persuade her to live in the Valley and marry him now. It was obvious she was going to do whatever her mother wanted her to do, no matter what; he decided he wouldn't go to the singings. John thought to himself, "I'm not going to keep company with anyone who doesn't care enough for me to do what is in her heart." So, John helped his Dad with the family's farm and spent all summer working on his little place. He would soon forget about Rose.

Betty Anne was working three days a week at the flower shop in the hospital and was exhausted when she got home every day. All she could do was to lie down for a while. Her heart had been giving her problems again, and she seemed to be out of breath a lot. Her neighbor would come over a couple of nights a week and bring her dinner. Betty Anne was so grateful to her neighbor Barbara, and told her that when she felt better, she was going to take her out to dinner.

Chapter Forty-Three

One afternoon in late summer of 1988, she received a letter from Sadie. She was coming to visit with Emily Grace. The child was walking now and talking up a breeze. Betty Anne was so excited that her chest started to hurt. She sat down in a chair and took some deep breaths as she started to feel a little better. She decided she'd better make an appointment with her heart doctor before the girls came, just to make sure everything was alright. She didn't want to be sick or unable to enjoy her visit while they were there.

She followed up with her appointment a couple of days later. The doctor said, "Your heart has gotten weaker, and you need to take it easy for a while." She said, "I lost my son, Danny almost a year ago, and I have been depressed since it happened." He replied, "All the grieving you have experienced over the years is not helping your heart." He added another pill for her to take and said, "Maybe you should go see a professional about the depression." She replied, "I've thought about going to see a professional, but I just don't have the time right now.

My daughter is coming for a visit next week. Maybe I can do that after she has gone home."

Sara Jane and Levi drove the buggy into town one day to pick up supplies for the farm. She said, "I need to stop by and see Betty Anne. I'll drop you off at the general store." She drove the buggy down the street until she came to Betty Anne's house. The car was parked in the driveway, so she got out and walked up to the door. When Betty Anne opened the door, she was elated to see Sara Jane standing there. She said, "Come on in the house, and have a cup of tea." She was delighted to see her friend, but she had been lying down and looked as white as a ghost. She was concerned and said, "I rode into town with Levi to pick up a few supplies from the general store today. I wanted to stop by and see how you were feeling." Betty Anne said, "Oh, I'm fine. I was just resting before you came. Sadie and the baby are coming for a visit, and I wanted to be rested up." That's wonderful news. I'm so happy for you, but I'm still concerned about your health. Have you been having problems with your heart again?"

"No, everything is fine. Please don't worry yourself about me."

Betty Anne tried to change the subject and spoke about how pretty Sara Jane's dress looked. She had on a dark blue Amish dress with a white starched apron and a white kappa.

She said, "Did you make the dress you are wearing, Sara Jane? The color is so pretty on you.

How is the quilting group doing?"

She knew Betty Anne was trying to get the subject off herself and just played along with her. She said, "The quilting group is doing fine at Maggie's house. The women miss you and wish you would come back. When are you coming back, Betty Anne? It would do you a lot of good to get involved with the quilting group again." Betty Anne was hesitant for a moment and said, "maybe when I feel better, emotionally." Sara Jane replied, "The ladies are working on another wedding quilt for one of the girls in the community." This interested Betty Anne, and she said, "maybe, after Sadie's visit I will to try to come. I truly loved working on the wedding quilts."

Sara Jane was overjoyed to hear her say that she might come back and couldn't wait to tell the other Amish women. She hoped that her friend would at least attempt to come back; it would do her a lot of good. She thought to herself, "Betty Anne needs to associate herself with other people. It would help her get over her depression. Sadie and the baby's visit will be good for her too."

After Sara Jane had been there for about an hour, she thought she'd better go and pick Levi up at the general store. They hugged and said goodbye, and she got in the buggy and guided the horse up the street. On the way home, she started thinking about Betty Anne and what she might do to help her. Quilting was the one thing that Betty Anne loved doing the most. She had to get her back in the quilting group again as soon as she can.

Betty Anne and Sadie had a wonderful visit with each other. Emily Grace was almost two years old and walking all over the place. Betty Anne started thinking, "Emily Grace is such a sweet child and reminds me of Sadie when she was a little girl. Sadie and Danny were a handful when they were small. Because they were twins, I would dress them alike as much as possible. Sometimes money was tight, and I just couldn't buy the clothes I wanted."

Betty Anne said, "Sadie, I need to explain a few things to you about your childhood."

They sat in the kitchen drinking coffee as Betty Anne talked to Sadie about her growing up years. "Being twins wasn't easy for you and Danny. When you were twelve years old, your father got called up to go to Vietnam with his army platoon. He was shot and killed by a sniper. Our lives were never the same after that. I had to go back to my nursing job and raise you two on my own. There wasn't much money, even though I did get a little from the army. But it was never enough. I worked long hours to make enough money to support the three of us. I tried to give you and Danny everything possible, but it just wasn't enough. You said you were embarrassed by me and hated me. As soon as you and Danny graduated from high school, you both left Ruby Hope Valley and told me you weren't ever coming back. I've wondered for years what I did wrong, and why you and Danny left me."

Chapter Forty-Four

Sadie had tears in her eyes as she sat there listening to her mother speak. She said, "Mother, I was a teenager, and I admit I was a selfish and uncaring one. I have always loved you, but my life just got tangled up in so many ways. I traveled around for while trying to find myself.

I was a wreck for a period. Then I met my husband, and my life changed." She reached out for her mother's hands and held them as she said, "I am so sorry I caused you to suffer all these years. Please forgive me, I won't ever leave you again." She got up from her chair and walked over to Betty Anne and put her arms around her.

Sadie noticed that her mother had lost weight and looked pale and tired. She said, "Mother, do you have any medical problems I need to know about?" Betty Anne replied, "I'm just getting old and tired." Sadie wasn't going to take that for an answer, so she decided she was going to ask her neighbor, Barbara, or maybe Sara Jane. She thought that surely one of them would know.

She was aware that her mother was not over the death of her twin brother, Danny, and that she could be suffering from depression. But she wondered if there was anything else going on, too. Sadie asked, "Do you feel like taking a ride out to the country to visit the Click family?"

"Yes, I'm fine, I would love to ride out there. Why don't we plan to go tomorrow?" Betty Anne replied. The following day they drove out to the house and surprised Sara Jane.

She welcomed them and invited them into the kitchen to have a piece of apple pie and a cup of hot tea. She could hardly believe how Emily Grace had grown and how adorable she was. She said, "She looks just like her Mother." You could see the proud expression on Betty Anne's face when she talked about Emily Grace. She was delighted to see the boys and hugged them to her chest.

They loved Betty Anne and considered her their grandmother. She loved them too and thought of them as her grandbabies as well. Sadie said, "Sara Jane, would you show me the rest of the house? Mother, do you feel like keeping an eye on Emily Grace?"

"Of course, I will, and you'll stay as long as you need too. Us girls will be fine."

Sadie had made up her mind to ask Sara Jane what was going on with her mother's health. The way she could was to get her away from her.

They walked upstairs and sat down on the bed. She knew that Sadie needed to ask her something, and she was prepared to tell her anything she asked. It was time Betty Anne's daughter knew the truth about her mother. Sara Jane said, "Sadie, your Mother had a heart valve operation a couple of months ago. I think she may be having problems again.

She gets tired and is depressed over Danny. Her heart just gets weaker and weaker, and the doctor wants her to slow down and maybe see a professional about the depression."

Sadie couldn't believe how her mother had kept all this to herself and didn't tell her about her heart. She felt guilty about staying away all those years; she felt in her heart that this illness was caused by her and Danny. Tears began to fall as Sara Jane filled her in on everything that had been happening over the past few years. Sadie thanked her for telling her about her Mother and gave her a hug. She said, "I am so glad my mother has you and your family in her life.

Sara Jane said, "I baked a chicken casserole and vegetable soup for lunch today. I'm hoping you'll stay and eat with us." Sadie said. "That sounds delicious Sara Jane; we'll stay if you are sure it's ok. Mother has told me what a good cook you are, and I can't wait to see for myself." Levi and Samuel came in for lunch and were glad to see Betty Anne. They sat down at the table as Levi lowered his head and said the silent prayer.

On the drive home Betty Anne was quiet, and Sadie asked, "Is anything wrong, Mother?"

"No, I'm just a little tired." Sadie was worried about her and decided to call her doctor when they got back home. She put the baby down for a nap, and Betty Anne laid down for a spell too. Sadie went outside and called the doctor's office on her cell phone.

The nurse said, "The doctor will be free around 4:30 if you would like to come by then." It was already 3:30 in the afternoon, so she thought she would ask Barbara if she would come over and stay during the time she was gone. She explained to her what she was up to, and she understood.

Chapter Forty-Five

Sadie drove over to the doctor's office and tried to speak with her mother's doctor.

He was reluctant to talk to her about her, but she told him that she was her single relative and she needed to know what was going on with Betty Anne's heart. The doctor thought about it and said, "I try to respect my patients' privacy, but since you are Betty Anne's daughter I can tell you most of her problem right now is depression. She had a heart valve operation in the last six months. She should be doing fine with her heart now. She needs something to keep her busy and give her an interest in life -- like a flower garden or volunteering a little of her time. All the grieving she did over losing her son weakened her heart and made the valve problem worse.

So, she had to have the operation. But it should be doing fine."

Sadie was heartbroken and thought about all the years they had lost, pointlessly out of touch. How selfish she had been just thinking of herself. She needed to make it up to her, but she wondered how she could do that. The weekend came, and it was time for Sadie and Emily Grace to go back to New York. She wasn't ready to leave her, but she had to go home. She said, "We will see you soon, Mother. Remember I love you." On the flight Sadie tried to think of anything she could do with her mother to make up for lost time. She thought of a cruise together, just herself and her mother. A four-day cruise to the Bahamas would be nice. She would truly love that.

After arriving home, she spoke with her husband and mother-in-law and told them her thoughts. They both agreed the cruise to the Bahamas was a wonderful idea. "We'll take good care of Emily Grace; you won't have to worry about her," her mother-in-law said. Sadie set about the preparations for the trip. She called Betty Anne and told her about the cruise and when they were going. Her mother was surprised and very excited about the trip and said she couldn't wait. Sadie said, "This trip is just for the two of us."

In August 1988 Sadie and Betty Anne left to go on their cruise together. They were both wildly excited and had knots in their stomachs. They got aboard the Fantasy ship in Orlando, Florida and Betty Anne was hoping she wasn't going to get sea sickness. Sadie was thinking how she wanted to rebuild the bond between her and her mother that had seemed lost many years ago.

The first night on the cruise they had dinner with the maître d'. During the time they were dining they could see the dolphins jumping in the water outside the window of the ship. Betty Anne said, "I am having such a good time already and wondering what is coming next." A man played the piano and sang a Frank Sinatra song. While he was singing, he was staring straight into Betty Anne's eyes. It gave her chills up and down her spine. She thought he had the most beautiful voice she had ever heard before. The next day they went to the casino, and she won two thousand dollars playing the slot machines. She was having the best time of her life.

But the most important part of the whole trip was being with Sadie.

They strolled along the deck of the ship with their arms around each other, talking about her win, and Sadie pointed out all the quilting martials she could get for the group now.

Betty Anne said, "That is an excellent idea. I plan on doing that when I get back to Ruby Hope." They saw two helicopters flying overhead. The helicopter crew were dropping pamphlets about a new restaurant in the Bahamas. Sadie said, "Look, this looks like a good place to eat. When we get to the island, let's try it out." The food on the menu sounded so good they could hardly wait. That evening, though, Betty Anne begin throwing up: she had sea sickness. Betty Anne scolded to herself, "Of all things, I had to get sick just when the ship is about to pull into port." Sadie brought her a little Dramamine for her sea sickness, and they hoped she would be ok. After taking the pills Betty Anne did begin to feel a little better. She wasn't going to miss out on the opportunity to visit the island. They had a fun day and decided to eat at that new restaurant.

They did a bit of souvenir shopping while drinking lattes and eating snacks such as candy from a quaint little shop. Betty Anne said, "I have decided to get Barbara a new scarf, but I'm not sure what to get Sara Jane." She bought a beautiful new scarf for Barbara; it had a lot of red, green, and blue in it. She said, "This scarf will look lovely with her red hair."

That evening they returned to the ship, and Betty Anne told Sadie she just had to rest a spell. Both the women decided to go to their cabins and took a nap. Even Sadie was tired after a day of walking and shopping all over the island. That evening they went to dinner in the main dining room. Betty Anne wanted to sit by the window, so she could watch the dolphins again. A nice looking older gentleman came over to the table and asked Betty Anne to dance. She had not danced in years but thought she would give it a try. He was very good looking for his age, but she wasn't interested in trying to get a man. She had too many other things in her life, and that was the last thing on her mind.

Chapter Forty-Six

The following day they had their pictures taken on the spiral staircase that was located right in the middle of the ship. She needed something to remember this wonderful trip with her daughter. Sadie said, "Mother, let's go swimming!" Betty Anne replied, "I think I will just lie in one of the lounge chairs and watch you swim." She had not had on a bathing suit in years. After Sadie finished swimming they decided to go shopping on the island again. They just had one more day there, and she thought she would get Sara Jane and her family a few gifts.

Betty Anne was feeling better than she had in a long time. She was a little tired but felt stronger and decided when she got back she was going to start getting out more and stop moping around the house.

Uncertain what to get for Sara Jane, she turned to her daughter for help. Sadie said, "A few yards of beautiful material for a dress would be nice for Sara Jane." Betty Anne understood that she loved purple, so she got her five yards of purple material. She said with satisfaction, "This is going to look great on Sara Jane, and now I think I will get Levi a new straw hat. The one he wears every day is torn in several different places. I believe I will get the boys a sack full of hard candies along with a cute little whistle."

That evening was the last night on the cruise, and they decided to do something fun, so they joined a karaoke bar. They got up on the stage together and sang the old song called "Sh Boom Sh Boom," written by the Crew Cuts in the fifties. They were so good that the audience was clapping and yelling and asking them to keep singing. They had a lot of fun that night, and Betty Anne felt like a young girl again. She didn't want the cruise to end because she knew her daughter would have to leave. She started missing her as soon as they got off the ship; but home she must go. The trip with Sadie was just what Betty

Anne needed. She had her daughter back in her life and Danny lived in her heart.

When she went back to her heart doctor for her checkup, he told her, "Your heart sounds a lot better. It's not as weak as it was before. I believe the cruise helped you more than you know. Your heart isn't healed, but it sounds a lot stronger. If you keep yourself busy and take your medications like you should, you should have a long life."

After she left the doctor's office, she began thinking, "I'm going to start going to the quilting group again and get involved with social things in town. Maybe get on a committee or taking up collections for a fund. Whatever it takes, to get my health back on track. I think I will start back to work in the flower shop too, but no more than two days a week. That way I would have time to join in on the quilting group again. I need to talk to Sara Jane to see if she will go with me to pick out material for the quilting group ladies."

She drove out to the farm a few days after coming back from her cruise with Sadie.

She decided to take Sara Jane and her family the gifts she had gotten them and ask her about the quilting material. As always, they insisted she must stay for dinner. They sat in the kitchen and had a cup of tea after dinner, as Betty Anne told them all about the trip. Joseph Levi and Samuel John were very excited to hear about the dolphins and kept asking her to tell the story over and over. She loved the purple material she gave her, but she knew Levi might not approve. Even though Betty Anne had been a part of the family for years now, he was still a little hesitant about accepting gifts from her.

Levi was a very strong Amish man who always stood by the rules of his faith. He knew with Betty Anne, even though she was a true Christian woman, he had to bend the rules. He loved her like family, but he was against all the gift giving. He knew Betty Anne had a good heart and meant no harm but was just doing what her faith had taught her all her life.

Their beliefs were different, but with Betty Anne, he just had to overlook some things. He could find no fault with her decision to spend her winnings on supplies for the quilting circle, though.

Betty Anne said, "Sara Jane, will you go with me to help pick out material for the quilting group?" They chose a day they could ride up to the big flea market.

Fall was in the air, and the weather was perfect for them to go to the market. Betty Anne was subsequently coming out of her depression, and she was delighted and relieved to see her like this. She had been so worried about her over the past few months. Betty Anne said,

"Sadie and I have created a new bond between us.

Chapter Forty-Seven

As they were sitting and talking, Levi ran in the back-door yelling, he needed help in the barn. Samuel had burned his arm on the hot hammer. They all ran out the back door and across the yard to the barn. Samuel was lying down on the ground with a cold cloth on his arm. Betty Anne said, "Levi, help get him up off the ground and bring him outside. Sara Jane, can you go call an ambulance for Samuel?" She ran as fast as she could down the road to the phone booth. She said, "the ambulance is on its way."

Samuel was taken to the hospital outside of Ruby Hope Valley and put in the burn unit.

He had third degree burns on his left arm. Levi sent word to Mattie Sue and then sat down in the waiting room with his hands over his face. He kept saying, "it's my fault, it's my fault." Betty Anne asked, "Can you tell us what happened?"

"We were working when the fire in the pit started raging high, I pulled back away from it with the hot hammer in my hand and bumped into Samuel. When I did the hammer came down on his arm." Sara Jane sat down beside him and put her arms around his shoulders as she tried to reassure him the accident wasn't his fault. She said, "Levi, it was an accident. It wasn't your fault."

After about two hours the doctor came out and said, "The burn isn't as bad as we thought to begin with. The scarring shouldn't be that noticeable when it heals." Levi was greatly relieved and said a silent prayer for his brother. Many of the Amish Community came to the hospital to check on Samuel and wanted to know if there was anything they could do to help. They all gathered around in the waiting room as the Bishop said a prayer for Samuel and his family. The nurses and doctors were once again amazed at how they always came together to help one another.

Samuel was released after a few days in the hospital. His arm was bandaged up to his shoulder, and he was worried about his brother having to do all the work by himself. Levi said, "Samuel don't worry about anything; just take care of that arm." They were very careful from then on, and Levi figured out a safer way to work with the hammer and the forge fire. He knew that Samuel and Mattie Sue were expecting another child after Christmas. He said. "I feel so guilty that Samuel is missing time off from work. Sara Jane, what do you think about reimbursing Samuel for his time off? She said, "I agree with you, Levi; you need to do what is in your heart."

Levi knew that his brother's family had to eat and take care of Ethan Nathaniel, plus another baby on the way. Samuel couldn't work his place, either. Levi said, "I'm going to give him several weeks' pay in hopes it will make things a little better for them. The Amish people went in together and paid Samuel's doctor bills. As always, they were there to support one of their own. The men in the community came over to Samuel's house every day he was out of work and took care of his animals and fields.

The women in the community brought casseroles, fried chicken, and several other dishes to Samuel's house during the time he was out of work. A few of the women came to their house to take care of Ethan Nathaniel whilst Mattie Sue took Samuel to follow up appointments and burn therapy. During the time she was gone, they would hang out the wash and clean the house for her.

Betty Anne wasn't surprised at all that the Amish people had stepped in to support Samuel and his family. She had seen their generosity many times through the years. The people of Ruby Hope Valley were almost as generous as their Amish neighbors. Someone was always there to help in times of sickness or sorrow. That was what Betty Anne loved the most about living in this place. The people made all the difference in this little town.

As time went by, Samuel was able to come back to work. Levi showed Samuel how he had perfected a new way to do the horseshoeing. It was a safer and cleaner technique.

Levi prayed what happened to Samuel would never happen again.

Chapter Forty-Eight

Christmas time had come once again to the Valley; it was December 1988. Snow was falling and covering everything in sight. As Betty Anne looked out the window she could see Christmas lights shining through the windows of the houses around her. She felt like a new person since the cruise. The trip with Sadie had helped to get her over her depression, and she was ready to live again. She had been in the depths of despair and hadn't wanted to live for a long time. She was now ready to get out and enjoy this beautiful holiday season. She decided it was time to get involved with the community as a volunteer. She had several places in mind.

Betty Anne was walking along Main Street one afternoon soon afterward, enjoying the Christmas decorations in the store windows when she came across a sign in one of the stores.

It was a picture of children in an orphanage. She had already had it in mind to see if she might be of service to orphans, and this touched her so much that she decided she would go to the local orphanage right away.

The children liked Betty Anne and thought of her as the grandmother type. She didn't mind that at all because she wanted them to be comfortable around her. They were getting ready to decorate a big tree that had been donated to them by the local Christmas tree society.

It had been placed in the big hall so that any visitors could see it as soon as they entered the building. The children were laughing and chatting to each other and excited about Christmas.

Several of them were going to spend the holidays with local families, and some had to stay at the group home. She felt sorry for the ones that had to stay behind. She said, "I wish there was some way I could make them all happy. I think I will help them decorate the tree and make all sorts of decorations." The kids had a lot of fun with her, and she enjoyed every minute of it.

She became very attached to the little ones and wanted to take them home with her. One little girl pulled at her heart strings, and she couldn't seem to get her out of her mind. She had blonde hair and blue eyes and was very small for her age, which Betty Anne guessed was about three or four. Her name was Daisy Mae, and she loved Betty Anne and clung to her whenever she was around. She reminded the woman a little of her granddaughter.

Becky White, the supervisor of the group home asked Betty Anne to come to her office a few days later. She told her about Daisy Mae's family. She realized how attached she was getting to the child and thought she should know how she came to be there. Ms. White said, "Miss Betty Anne, I know you are getting attached to Daisy, so I thought I would fill you in on her background. Maybe you can be of some help to these children." She told the older woman that Daisy had one brother, Jacob, who was ten, and a sister, Cindy, seven. Their mother had been a prostitute and neglected them severely. She beat the kids and left them unattended for days on end. They were starving, filthy, and didn't have milk for the baby when the police found them.

Daisy was that baby. She was dehydrated and malnourished when they were found.

One of the women downstairs had reported the mother to the local police. She would see her leaving every night and knew the kids were left abandoned. She heard them crying and sometimes screaming from the abuse, the mother put on them, and the baby seemed to cry all the time. At first, she didn't know what to do because she was afraid the mother might come after her. They already had a few run ins with each other, so she stayed quiet for a long time. Then it got cold, and she saw the boy out running around with scarcely anything on to keep him warm.

She just couldn't stand it any longer and contacted the local police.

When they were found, they were filthy and starving. There was no heat and very little food in the apartment. Daisy was in a crib wearing a dirty diaper that had not been changed in a couple of days. The poor child had blisters on her little bum. It was the worst case of neglect the policeman had ever seen. That officer couldn't sleep at night for thinking about those kids. They had been brought to the orphanage from Pittsburgh. She finished by saying" We have done everything within our power to help them. They have trust issues, except Daisy, of course. She was so small at the time she doesn't remember anything."

Betty Anne had not been able to keep the tears back, and she wanted to know what happened to their mother. Becky said, "The last I heard, she was locked up for child endangerment." When Betty Anne went to her house that night, she sat for a long time in her recliner and thought about those kids. She said aloud to the empty room "How in the world could a Mother do that to her children?" She just couldn't get over it and had a hard time getting to sleep that night.

She kept thinking about Daisy and how she wished she could find her a loving home.

Then unexpectedly, she thought about Sara Jane and Levi. She wanted a little girl and couldn't have any more children, so Daisy would be perfect for them; and maybe, just maybe the other two could go too.

Chapter Forty-Nine

The more Betty Anne considered it, the more she liked the idea. But, she thought, how in the world am I going to get Sara Jane to meet the kids? She decided she would try to get her friend to volunteer at the orphanage with her. She drove out to the farm the next day and told her that she had been volunteering at the local group home. She said, "Sara Jane, we could actually use your help there. There are so many children who need us; and they are really shorthanded."

Sara Jane said, "I truly would like to, Betty Anne, but I need to talk with Levi first. He may not want me to become a volunteer."

Given that it was Christmas, Sara Jane truly wanted to volunteer at the orphanage. Levi understood she had been having a hard time over the last few months. The hysterectomy and her grandpa passing away had made her sad. He said, "Sara Jane, I don't mind you becoming a volunteer, but you will need to find someone to watch the boys while you're gone. I'm too busy in the barn to watch them." She said, "Mattie Sue said she would be happy to watch them two days a week." He was satisfied with the idea of the boys staying with Samuel's wife and told her to go ahead. She was very excited and couldn't wait to tell Betty Anne.

The first thing Betty Anne did was to introduce her to Daisy, Jacob, and Cindy. Sara Jane fell in love with Daisy. The child was shy and consistently clung to Betty Anne. When she went home that night, she told Levi about Daisy and her brother and sister. She instantly wanted to bring them home for Christmas. He was totally against the idea and said, "Sara Jane, those kids might have a hard time going back to the home after Christmas. You need to think about that before you bring them to the farm."

She was disappointed with his answer but knew better than to disagree with him. She went back the following day and tried to stay away from the children as much as she could. That was the hardest thing she ever had to do? Betty Anne knew that Sara Jane would love Daisy, but she didn't want the kids to be separated. Betty Anne was hoping he would give in sooner or later.

She felt that if Sara Jane took the children for Christmas, she would be reluctant to carry them back.

Levi could see the look on Sara Jane's face each time she came home from the orphanage. She had a sad look and didn't have much to say. He said, "I thought that volunteering at the home would help you feel less sad, but now I am concerned that you seem worse. You should stop going to the orphanage and forget about those kids." She began crying and said, "But Levi, I can't stop thinking about Daisy. I wish you would go with me one time. You could meet Daisy and her sister and brother." She wore him down, and he said, "If it will make you happy, I will go one time." Sara Jane told her friend the next day, "Betty Anne, I am so excited. Levi has agreed to come to the orphanage one time with me. I want him to meet the children." Betty Anne realized her plan was working now and said a silent prayer thanking God. She felt if he met the kids he would agree to let them stay with them over Christmas. Then it was just a matter of time before they would want to adopt them? Every time she thought about what those children went through, she could hardly stand it; it broke her heart.

On the Monday before Christmas, Sara Jane and Levi went to the group home to see the children. Betty Anne was already there waiting for her friend. She was surprised to see Levi and so proud of him for coming. He sat in the corner of the big main hall and watched the children run and play around the Christmas tree. Betty Anne and Sara Jane were playing games with them, and the kids were hanging all over them. They loved these two women and looked ahead to them coming each week. One of the little girls, whose name was Kathy, asked Sara Jane if she was coming back after Christmas. She said, "Please come back! We will all miss you if you don't." She didn't know what to say and said, "I will try my best to come back." Kathy was happy with that answer and ran off to play with the other girls.

Sara Jane brought Daisy over to meet Levi, but she was a little shy and clung to her as she tried to put her down. Levi said, "Hello, Daisy. You are a very pretty girl. Sara Jane said you were very sweet." She hid her face with her hands. Later, when they discussed the day, he said, "I still don't think it's a good idea to take Daisy and her brother and sister home. What if she cries, and the other two kids don't get along with the boys?" She tried to assure him that Daisy would be just fine, and she would look after all of them.

Chapter Fifty

Levi didn't want the responsibility, but at last agreed to let the children come for Christmas. The two women were exultant when he agreed to let them go to the farm. Betty Anne said, "Jacob, you and your sisters are going home with the Clicks.

They live on a farm, and you will have lots of fun playing with their two little boys." Daisy grabbed her around the neck and hugged her as tight as she could. Jacob and Cindy didn't have much to say. They had trust issues with people but felt secure at the home because nobody bothered them or hurt them. Sara Jane said, "I assure you we will have lots of fun on the farm. We have horses and cows in the barn. And nobody will ever hurt you again."

Sara Jane told the three children she needed to talk with Mrs. White and would be back tomorrow to pick them up. Daisy laughed, got down off her and ran to play with the other kids. Betty Anne and Sara Jane just stood there looking at her, and then she turned to her friend and said, "Thank you. Thank you for bringing me here and finding Daisy." Betty Anne wanted to tell Levi and Sara Jane the story Mrs. White told her about Daisy and her siblings but thought it could wait until another day. Her friend was going to take Daisy and her brother and sister home with her; that's what mattered.

The following day, the Clicks hitched up the horses to the buggy and headed toward town. The orphanage was located right on the edge of town. She had knots in her stomach and was a little nervous. he said, "Sara Jane, what happens if you decide you want to keep these kids. What then? She looked at him and said, "Maybe we could foster them until a family is found for them. I don't want to see them separated. I just know these kids have been through a lot in their young lives. I want to find out what happened to them." Levi knew in his heart before they ever left the house that these kids would never go back to the orphanage.

The three children came to the farm for Christmas. Joseph Levi and Samuel John loved playing with the kids. They seemed to get along with each other except for Jacob. He sat on the front porch and wouldn't speak to anyone at first. Joseph Levi said. "Jacob would you like to go see the horses? We have some new baby kittens, too." Jacob's face lit up as he followed Joseph Levi to the barn. Jacob loved the animals. Sara Jane had made Daisy and Cindy little Amish dolls. The girls carried them wherever they went in the house.

Mindful that Christmas was just three days away, she decided to make Daisy and Cindy an Amish dress. She planned the Christmas dinner and did some baking before she begins sewing. She made each one of them a little purple Amish dress with a white apron, then she put a cot in their bedroom, right next to their bed, for Daisy and Cindy. She was afraid they might get scared in the night, and she needed to be near them if they did.

Levi didn't like the idea of the two girls sleeping in their room; he was hoping it was temporary. Daisy and Cindy slept next to the couple's bed with their arms around their little dolls. She laid there in bed watching them sleep. She thought Daisy and Cindy were precious girls; She prayed they would never have to carry them back to that home again. It was a decent place, she reflected, and the people that worked there tried to make the kids happy?

She could see, but it was hard in such circumstances to help them one on one. The little ones like Daisy and Cindy needed a lot of love and affection. Jacob had seemed to get along with Joseph Levi and Samuel John as the day had worn on, and unknown to her, he slept better that night than he had in a long while.

Betty Anne was once again invited to Christmas Dinner and was looking in advance to it. The weather had been bad for a time but seemed to be clearing up now. The beautiful Christmas lights that lined Main Street were exceptionally lovely this year. She decided she would get out and enjoy the nice crisp air. She put on her hat, gloves, and boots. She wound a scarf around her neck and went shopping.

Chapter Fifty-One

This year she felt a new beginning in her life. She decided that after the holidays, she would quit her job at the flower shop and devote as much time as she could to the children at the orphanage. As she drove out to the farm, she reflected that those kids had been through so much. She thought it was time to tell her friends about the children's past. Perhaps another Amish family in the community might want to adopt Cindy and Jacob. After all, the boy was just the right age to help with the farm duties and learn all about the animals.

Cindy could be a lot of company for the Mother.

When she arrived at the farm, the kids ran out to greet her and threw their arms around her. Even Daisy, Cindy, and Jacob came out to see her. The girls looked adorable in their new purple Amish dresses. She had pulled their hair back in little buns on their heads. Betty Anne was so happy to see these five kids and wrapped her arms around them all at once. Sara Jane said, "Ruth is too feeble to come and stayed at the farm with Caleb and Maggie this year; but Dad and John are coming. Grandpa is going to be missed this year too."

They had a wonderful Christmas dinner with roast turkey, gravy, mashed potatoes, and green beans. She had also been up to her baking again, and offered Betty Anne her favorite, apple pie. She had also baked a chocolate cake and blueberry muffins.

Daisy was a sweet child and sat at the table without making a sound. She held on to that little Amish doll as if someone might grab it away from her. Cindy and Jacob were very quiet too and didn't eat very much. She was worried about them but just figured they were still a little scared.

After dinner Sara Jane and Betty Anne sat at the kitchen table and talked about the orphanage and Daisy. The men folks went into the sitting room and talked about the farm and the animals. Sara Jane said, "Betty Anne, I actually would love to keep Daisy. I'm afraid to approach Levi with the idea. I don't know what to do. I need your help." Betty Anne nodded. "I will try to talk to him soon and get his thoughts about Daisy. Do you know an Amish family that might want to foster or adopt Jacob and Cindy?" Sara Jane replied, "I wish we could keep them. But I'm afraid he wouldn't want to do that." Betty Anne said, "I wish the children didn't have to be separated at all. But I can understand how it would put a burden on your family to go from two kids to five."

Betty Anne thought that maybe this was a good time to tell them about the children's history. After Mark and John left to go, she decided to talk to Levi and Sara Jane about the kids.

She figured if they heard about their past it might make a difference. When they sat in the kitchen listening to Betty Anne, she told them, "These three youngsters have had a rough past, and I hesitated to tell you about it. But I think now is the time." They sat quiet, and she said, "Their mother was a prostitute, so they probably don't have the same fathers.

They lived in an upstairs apartment with no heat and very little food. The mother went out at night and left Jacob in charge of the two girls. Daisy was just a baby in a crib then.

The lady downstairs had several run-ins with their mother and was afraid to speak up.

But when she saw Jacob out in the freezing cold with hardly anything on to keep him warm, she finally called the police. When they came out to investigate, they were horrified at what they found." The couple felt shock as they listened to her. She continued. "There was no heat in the apartment, so Cindy and Jacob were huddled up together in a corner of the dark room. Daisy was in the crib crying with a nasty diaper on. The authorities think it had not been changed in several days. Her little bum had blisters on it." Sara Jane began to cry. He took her hand. It was going to be hard to take them back to the foster home now.

Chapter Fifty-Two

Two days after Christmas it was time to for the kids to return to the foster home, and Sara Jane was heartbroken. She truly loved all three of them and didn't think she was going to be able to carry them back. She called Becky White and said, "Mrs. White, I don't think we are going to be able to bring the children back until this weather gets better. We need to wait a couple of days. It's drizzling and cold, and the roads are too hazardous for our horses."

Mrs. White said, "Of course, I understand, Mrs. Click. You can wait until the weather lets up to bring them back."

There were rules and regulations governing the orphanage, but the organization in Ruby Hope was a little laid back. The staff just wanted what was best for the kids. Mrs. White was always hoping she could find each child a good home.

Betty Anne was happy they could keep them a couple more days. She decided she would try and talk to Levi about the children. Meantime, when she was at the group home one afternoon, she said, "Becky, is there any chance of Daisy, Jacob, and Cindy being adopted together? Sara Jane loves the kids, Becky, but she isn't sure her husband is willing to take them all in." Becky White said, "I have always had a dream of the children being adopted together. But most of the them get separated into different places.

After hearing the story of the children's past, Sara Jane just couldn't take them back to the orphanage. She said, "What if one of them gets adopted out and the other two are left behind?"

"I'm still not sure about all this, Sara Jane, but I know these kids need a good environment with people who love them. They have been through too much in their short lives."

"Daisy and Cindy have filled an emptiness I have felt since I found out I couldn't have any more babies."

He subsequently agreed to go and talk with Mrs. White about keeping the kids as soon as the weather got better. She thanked him profusely, saying, "Levi, I love you and thank you for letting the children come into our home."

It was after the new year had begun before Betty Anne could get back to the foster home. The weather was much better, so she decided to talk with Mrs. White about the children again. She said.

"Becky, my friends, the Clicks were talking about adopting all three of the kids. I finally told them about the youngsters' past, and my friend couldn't stop crying. They would rather they not be separated from each other." Mrs. White agreed and said, "I'm confident it will work out, for the children's sake."

The Clicks returned the children to the group home and told them not to worry, they were going to see if they could come and live with them permanently. They all smiled and hugged goodbye. The Clicks had made an appointment with Mrs. White and told her that they had decided to adopt the three children. She had them fill out the paperwork and told them that she had never had an Amish family adopt before. She said she would do all she could to help them and would let them know something as soon as she could. In the meantime, they were welcome to visit the children whenever they wanted. She knew she thought the world of the young couple, and she felt sure that with them the kids would have a loving home.

It took almost two months before they heard back from the foster home. Sara Jane had been volunteering there three days a week and spending as much time as she could with the three kids. Jacob was almost two years older than Joseph Levi, but they got along real well together and became best buddies. Samuel John and Cindy played games together and followed each other around a lot. Daisy was a mommy's girl and loved her. When they did take them back to the home, it was one of the hardest things they had ever done.

The day came when Mrs. White sent a letter to the Click family to come in to see her.

She had gotten an answer for them and wanted to share it in person. She called Betty Anne and Said, "Would you like to come in and be with the Click family today?" Betty Anne was nervous and tried to stay as calm as she could. She worried that because they were Amish, their request might be turned down. They all arrived at the same moment and went in to see Mrs. White.

She told them that the adoption board had agreed to let them take the kids on a trial basis for three months. If things worked out to their expectations, they would be able to adopt the kids. They were disappointed in the answer but agreed to keep the kids for three months.

Sara Jane was certain they would let them keep them after a while.

Chapter Fifty-Three

They took them home that very day, and Jacob joined his foster brothers to help their Dad on the farm. Joseph Levi and Jacob specifically loved helping in the barn. Jacob loved the animals as much as Joseph Levi and was willing to do anything Mr. Click needed him to do.

He learned how to milk the cows and feed the chickens. He would go out to the barn every day and brush the horses down for him. Joseph Levi would rake the stalls and fill the water buckets for the animals. Dad told them they had done a day's work and they were free to go and play a spell before dinner. The boys would go climb trees. Levi had found an old tire lying on the side of a road and took it home to make the kids a swing. They would take turns swinging, with never a cross word.

Jacob had subsequently opened-up and started acting like a normal boy. He loved being on the farm and being around people who cared about him. At night he would dream about the cold dirty apartment, he lived in and his mother beating him with a stick. He would moan and talk in his sleep and wake up sweating. When he woke up and looked around he was so thankful he was just dreaming again.

After the three months' period since the kids came home with them had almost elapsed, Mrs. White called Betty Anne and told her that she needed all of them to come in to see her in a week. The Clicks had a visit from the social workers, who had filed their recommendations. Next week would be the official end of the probationary period, and the decision could be made.

The youngsters had gotten used to being on the farm and living with the Clicks, so Jacob was worried that they might have to go back to the group home. Mr. Click loaded everyone up in the buggy and headed for the orphanage. Mrs. Click told the kids that no matter what happened that day, "Remember we love you." Jacob laid his head on Sara Jane's shoulder, and Cindy and Daisy got as close to her as they could, all the while holding onto their little Amish dolls.

When they arrived, they saw Betty Anne waiting for them at the door. They all walked into the orphanage together to see Mrs. White. She told them that she needed to ask the children a few questions. She asked Jacob how he liked living on the farm with the Click family. He said he loved being on the farm, and they had been good to him. She wanted to know if being Amish bothered him in any way. He said no, they were good folks and good to him. She asked him if he would like to live in the Amish neighborhood from now on. Jacob told her that living on an Amish farm had been fun, and he loved taking care of the animals. She asked Cindy how she felt about the Clicks. Cindy said she remembered her other mother and the way they had to live, and she realized these two people loved her, and that was all that mattered.

Mrs. White jotted something down on a piece of paper and then looked up at the Clicks and said, "The board has consented for you to adopt these three children." They looked at each other in relief and began hugging and crying all at the same moment. Betty Anne even cried, she was so happy. The three kids put their arms around the couple as if they would never let go of them.

Mrs. White said, "The children can go back with you today," and they all started jumping up and down with happiness. She couldn't wait to tell Dad and John. They gathered the children and took them to the farm.

Betty Anne decided to drive out to the farm and celebrate with them. Sara Jane told her she was going to fix a good dinner for everyone and invite Mark, John, Samuel, Mattie Sue, and little Ethan to come. She was hopeful that Grandmother Ruth would feel up to coming over for dinner, too. She put on a pot roast, boiled potatoes, green beans and squash. She had been baking as usual and already had an apple pie, sweet potato pie, and a coconut cake.

Betty Anne sat in the sitting room with the kids and read them a book about the Amish people. Little Daisy laid on the sofa with her head in Betty Anne's lap. Cindy sat on the floor with the boys as they listened closely. Jacob was trying to understand everything she was reading, but it was difficult because he had never met Amish people before Sara Jane and Levi. It wasn't long before Mark, John, Samuel, Mattie Sue, and the baby drove up in their buggies. They all sat down to a delicious dinner as Mark said the silent prayer. Samuel and Mattie Sue gave all the kids a big hug and told them how happy they were to have them there with them.

As time went by the three adopted kids began to feel right at home on the Amish farm.

Jacob and Joseph Levi got up early every morning and went to school together. After school they would head straight to the barn to help Levi and Samuel with the chores, never complaining about anything. Jacob felt deeply grateful to these people for taking him and his two sisters into their family. He was half afraid they would be separated one day and never see each other again. He understood he could never forget his past life with his real mother. He loved Sara Jane and felt that she was his mother now. She was as much his mother as anyone could be. She showed her love for these kids as much as her own. Joseph Levi and Samuel John were taught to never be envious of anyone else and to be grateful for all they had.

Chapter Fifty-Four

Sara Jane didn't mind taking care of the extra three children because she adored them. She felt so much happiness in making them clothes and brushing the girl's hair back into little buns. She cut Jacob's hair for him and got him a straw hat to wear. She gave him a book about the Amish religion and beliefs so he could learn more about them. He said,

"Thank you, for the book. I am determined to learn all about the Amish faith and the people." Jacob didn't mind wearing the hat because all the boys in the area wore straw hats, so he didn't feel out of place. He wore that straw hat with pride and dignity, and when the other boys would ask him questions about his past, he simply said "That was long ago. I don't want to talk about it."

Betty Anne couldn't have been happier for the young couple. She loved them so much and thought how wonderful for her. She has two little girls now. As she drove home that night she felt blessed to have such friends as these two people. They realized those kids needed to stay together, and they were willing to give them a home. Now she could see them whenever she wanted to.

She decided to continue volunteering at the group home at least three days a week. She thought that maybe she could start finding other homes for the kids. That would be a big job for her but would also give her a purpose in life, and that's what she needed the most: a purpose to get up every day and have some place she needed to be.

Betty Anne wanted to continue going to the quilting group too and decided that maybe she could get her quilting friends to help her make a nice quilt for her daughter. She decided to stop by the fabric store and pick out several nice pieces of material and share them with the quilting women. They all thought the pieces were beautiful for someone not Amish. They were bright colors.

Between the home group and the quilting group, Betty Anne's hands were full. But she liked keeping busy and thought she would see if the quilting ladies would let her friend join the group. She understood Barbara would love to learn how to quilt and would be willing to go with her. She asked the women if they would mind if she brought another Christian lady with her when she came. They were hesitant at first, but since it was for Betty Anne they all agreed it would be acceptable. Barbara joined the quilting group. She caught on fast and enjoyed quilting.

She could hardly wait to go again.

Soon after that, Betty Anne had to go back to her heart doctor. She had already gone and gotten her blood work, so she just needed to see how it turned out. The doctor said, "I am impressed with you. I can't believe all the things you are involved in. You have made a remarkable recovery, but I almost think you might have taken on too much." She told him about her friends adopting the three abused kids from the group home and how she helped it happen.

He was surprised and glad for the children and said, "I pray they will be happy now. Betty Anne, your heart seems stronger now, but you still need to slow down." Her blood pressures wasn't real high, but high enough that she needed to be sure to take all her meds every day. He said he wanted to see her again in two months.

After leaving the doctor's office she thought she would stop by the cemetery and see her son, Danny. She talked to him as if he was standing right there in front of her. She told him how much she loved him and how she found three orphans a new home. She told him how she had learned to quilt and was making Sadie a beautiful quilt. She ultimately told him how much she missed him and how she prayed every day for eight years for him to come home. But not this way, not in a coffin.

Chapter Fifty-Five

On the way home, she couldn't help but shed a few tears. She thought how funny it was the way things turn out. She wondered when she would see her daughter again. It had been at least two weeks since she called her.

When she got home she would call Sadie and see how things were. She wanted to hear Emily Grace jabber on the phone and to tell Sadie about the kids. She wanted to tell her that she had a good check up from the heart doctor. She had so many things to talk about and couldn't wait to talk to her.

Sadie was happy to hear her mother's voice on the phone. She put Emily Grace on the phone to talk to grandmamma. The child tried to talk to her, but she couldn't understand what she was saying, so she just talked back to her as if she did. She said, "Sadie, I just thought I would call to tell you about all the things that have happened. Sara Jane and Levi got to adopt the children. Oh, they are so happy and still celebrating. I have decided to volunteer three days a week at the orphanage. And I am going to the quilting group again.

My neighbor, Barbara is going with me now. The women agreed to let her come. The doctor says my heart is stronger too. So, between the quilting group and the group home, I'm going to be very busy." Sadie was happy for her Mother, and said, "I am so proud of you for keeping busy and doing the things you love to do."

"I feel very good these days and wished you would come to see me soon." Sadie said, "I will as soon as I can. My job is taking a lot of my time these days. I will try to get a few days off."

Betty Anne was satisfied with that and told her she loved her and hoped to see her soon. They hung up, and she felt a tear roll down her face as she always did whenever she talked to her daughter. She missed her so much and prayed she would come to see her soon.

The summer months promised to be very hot in the Valley, and Betty Anne didn't think she could stand it much longer. She had decided to plant a small garden in her back yard, so she went into town to the local nursery and bought several pots of flowers and vegetable seeds. She got down on her hands and knees and dug the dirt up out of the ground. She planted tomatoes, squash, cucumbers, and green beans on one side of the yard. Then she decided to get one of the local boys to come over and make a path between the vegetable garden and the flower garden.

She wanted to create a beautiful space for herself. After the boy finished with the path, she asked him to move a bench for her. The flower garden on the other side of the yard was just beautiful.

The daffodils were finished for the season, but it was full of lilies, roses, and dahlias. She had planted almost every kind of flower there was.

Her garden was so beautiful she decided to give it a name. She said out loud, "I think I will call this place 'Serenity.' That is a perfect name for my new space." She worked on it more and more, and Serenity garden became the talk of the town. People from all over the Valley came to see it and shoot pictures. She was so surprised, but she realized once the word got out around town, this would happen.

The people of Ruby Hope had heard about her good work at the group home too. She soon became somewhat of a local celebrity. People would stop her on the street and ask her about the three youngster's that were adopted by the Amish family. She would smile and say,

"Those kids are so lucky to be adopted by the Click family. They are wonderful people, and now the kids have a bright future ahead of them."

One lovely June afternoon, she was sitting on the bench in her garden when she heard someone say "grandmamma" in a sweet little voice. She turned around, and there stood Sadie and Emily Grace. She was so surprised and happy to see them and went over and hugged them both. Little Emily Grace said "grandmamma" again as she picked her up, and she couldn't help but cry. She seemed to cry at the drop of a hat these days; she just couldn't help it.

She thought to herself, I guess I'm just getting old. She didn't even know they were coming to visit her, but she was glad they did. They went into the house and sat in the kitchen as she put a pot of coffee on. She sat Emily Grace down at the table and gave her a couple of cookies and a small glass of milk. She suddenly remembered that she had purchased a little sippy cup for her a while back. She poured the milk into the sippy cup, so Emily Grace wouldn't spill it.

They sat in the kitchen for a long while talking about all the things that had been happening since Sadie's last visit. She was very pleased to see her feeling good and being active in the community. She knew things had been hard for her over the past year. She truly believed the cruise they took back in the fall had done her a world of good.

Sadie said, "I hear you are quite a celebrity around town these days.

Everyone is talking about you and those kids. How's the family? How are they, since the adoption?" She said. "All the children seem to be getting along together. Jacob, Cindy, and Daisy are adjusting to their new home. She is having a good time taking care of the girls. At the same time, Levi and Samuel are taking care of the boys. Jacob is learning the Amish ways and seems to be fitting in with the other kids. He took care of his little sisters when his mother was gone, and now he seems to be taking care of these kids too. Joseph Levi and he are big buddies and do everything together now. Samuel John and Cindy have become close playmates too. They are almost the same age, so they get along with each other very well.'

Sadie said, "You are a miracle worker and such a sweet lady. I can't believe I left you the way I did. I must have been a very selfish girl. Now all I want to do is make it up to my dear sweet Mother."

Chapter Fifty-Six

Betty Anne was getting up in age now but still seemed to have the energy to do the things she loved. And she loved volunteering at the group home and working in her garden.

She said, "Sadie, I have found five new homes for the group home kids, and they all have worked out wonderful."

"I am so impressed by this and so proud of you. That is the most amazing thing, I have ever heard."

Emily Grace began to get a little grumpy, so Sadie went to put her down for a nap. They had a long trip, and the child was tired. After she fell asleep, they continued to talk as she made them some lunch. She had made chicken salad that morning and vegetable soup. They laughed and cried and wore themselves out just talking about everything and everybody. They had such fun that day, and she said, "Mother, I will never forget this moment with you." Betty Anne said, "I will never forget the cruise either; thank you for taking me, Sadie."

One afternoon before Sadie and Emily Grace left to go back to New York, they all rode out to see the family. On the way out to the country, they noticed the green fields and beautiful flowers blooming. The men and their sons were out on their tractors planting or taking care of their chores around their homes. Sadie said, "I can understand how you love these people. There's a serene and comfortable feeling about this place, and even I can feel it." Betty Anne replied, "Their simple lives are happy ones, and they care for their own and their people. They are always there for one another."

As they drove down the dirt roads they came across a farm at which several Amish men were attempting to raise a barn. she said, "See Sadie, the men and women of their society come together for one another when they are needed. They help build barns and houses and whatever a neighbor needs. You know for a while I had thought of joining their faith. I was afraid of what you and Danny might think." Sadie said, "Now that I know them, I don't believe I would mind if you joined their people. I know how much you love Sara Jane and her family, and maybe that would be a good thing for you, Mother. You would never be lonesome again because these people tend to watch after each other and are always there when you need them."

They had a good visit with Sara Jane and the family that day. Sadie was in awe of the kids they had adopted and said, "Sara Jane, you are so lucky you found them." She replied to her, "If it had not been for your mother, we would have never known about the kids." Sadie Said, "God knows your heart, and he knew you needed these kids and they needed you and Levi. That's why he led you to them." She responded, "Yes, he knows our hearts, and I have prayed to have another child. But I guess I wasn't supposed to for this reason. Now I have two girls, and I love them all very much."

On the way home, the two women were silent for a long time. When they finally spoke, they both agreed that these people did the right thing for those kids. "Like I said mother, you are a miracle worker. You are a very special person, and I will never be too far away from you again if you need me." Betty Anne's heart was spilling over with emotion right then, and she couldn't help but shed some more tears. She thought to herself, "I am always crying about something."

Time came for Sadie and Emily Grace to leave, and she thought her heart was going to break. She tried to hold back the tears as she hugged and kissed them both goodbye.

Sadie didn't want to leave her again but knew she had to get back to her husband and job. She said, "I promise to call you, at least twice a week from now on. If you ever need me, pleased don't hesitate to call."

Emily Grace grabbed her grandmother around the neck and gave her a big kiss on her ' face. She thought that was the sweetest thing and could hardly let go of the child. They left, and she felt a little let down, but knew in her heart that she loved her and was back in her life for good.

Betty Anne continued to work with the kids at the orphanage. Her nursing skills played a big part in her life now. She would tend to the kids when they came down with a fever and could instantly recognize common illnesses such as strep throat or ear infections. She felt responsible for the kids there and wanted to help them in any way she could. She brought toys and clothes for them. She even read stories to them at bedtime. She knew in her heart that if she had not volunteered there, Sara Jane and Levi would never have known about Jacob, Cindy, and Daisy. It was an intervention from God, she knew that now.

She decided she would go water her flowers and see what the next day would bring. She said, "If the Lord is willing, I will get up tomorrow and find a child a home. And I will continue to love the people in my life. Oh, what a life it has been for me. I pray I will be here to see all these kids grow up and have fantastic lives. God has given me so many good friends and family, and I have no complaints." She said a silent prayer:

Thank you, Lord, for today and all the days ahead. Thank you for all the blessings you have bestowed on me. Amen.

Credits

Wikipedia – Note: Oak and the issues of cross contamination with wheat

DaVita – Note: Kidney Education Menu – Arteriovenous/fistula

Medicine Net – Script: Note: Creatinine in the Blood

The National Kidney Foundation: Note: Immunosuppressant/Anti-Rejection drugs

Abstract/Article Extract/Internet: Note: Transplantation in Children

The National Kidney Foundation: Note: Dialysis

Wikipedia / Ram springe

Amish America News: Note: What do the Amish eat?

A Poem Written by Sabrina A. Hernandez / My Little Boy

A Poem Written by Esther Keim / October 4, 2017 / My Children

Photos by Ronda Moss Photography/Atlanta, Georgia

Amish Boy – Ethan T. Moss

Amish Boy – Joshua E. Anderson

Amish Girl – Jo Marie Simms
Edited by Hester L. Furey/Atlanta Georgia

Thank you so much for reading one of our **Crime Fiction** novels.
If you enjoyed the experience, please check out our recommended title for your next great read!

Caught in a Web by Joseph Lewis

"This important, nail-biting crime thriller about MS-13 sets the bar very high. One of the year's best thrillers." *–BEST THRILLERS*

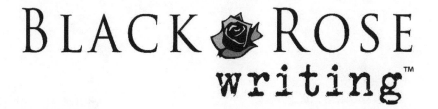

CPSIA information can be obtained
at www.ICGtesting.com
Printed in the USA
LVHW091942021218
599025LV00001B/218/P